DIRTY SECRET

A Slayers Hockey Novel

MIRA LYN KELLY

DIRTY SECRET

Photographer: WANDER AGUIAR PHOTOGRAPHY LLC

Cover Designer: Najla Qamber, Najla Qamber Designs

Editor: Jennifer Miller

For Jessica Alcazar

Chapter 1

Vaughn

*W*hat's pissing me off isn't the phone call from my agent warning me that Coach is going to scratch me from the lineup if I don't knock off my "confrontational" bullshit.

It's not that I walk into Belfast, the one bar I like in this city, and find Greg fucking Baxter and half our team cheering for some chump as he pops the question to his girl.

It's not even that I can't get a fucking beer because all the waitresses are standing around moony-eyed, or that any plans I might have had of getting laid tonight are now securely in the shitter. Trusting my dick to some chick who just watched a happily ever after in action? Hard pass. Might as well cut the hole in the rubber myself.

No. What's pissing me off is *her*, and that for a single second *I wasn't pissed at all*.

For one second, my only thought was *she's here*.

In Chicago.

In the bar I've been coming to once a week for the past month and a half.

Allie. The girl from Vancouver eight months ago. The one with the dark curls, gypsy blue eyes, and the sweetest, wettest mouth I ever tasted. The girl who blew my mind and then blew out of my life without even giving me her number.

Hell, I was half off my barstool, the beginnings of an honest-to-fuck smile fighting my chronic case of resting prick face when it registered... *She's not alone.*

And it's not some random hipster or suit with his arm slung around her shoulders, either. It's Ruxton Meyers, my teammate. Fucking Baxter's best friend.

That's what's pissing me off.

I thought she was *different*.

Hell, I knew she was a fan. She was wearing a Canucks jersey and hanging out at a bar with a bunch of players the first night I saw her. But she wasn't on the prowl. She wasn't eyeing every player there like a prize to score. Instead of some skintight getup that left next to nothing to the imagination, she'd had on jeans. Beat-up, loose, frayed-around-the-hems jeans. And a pair of white Chucks. Her hair was this sexy mess of dark brown waves that I watched her put up into a ponytail in the middle of the bar without a mirror, *while she was talking to another player*. She didn't care what she looked like. Didn't care what anyone thought. Didn't even have her phone out taking selfies.

So not a puck bunny.

I'd have bet my life on it, especially when I saw her in the hotel lobby the next night. She was buying a Hershey's bar and a lemonade from the convenience store and she just looked up and smiled. Like we were old friends or something. Like she recognized me without the double take. Without the rest of the team. Just me, standing in line behind her buying a water I didn't need because I'd seen her there.

And hours later when I could still smell her on my skin, the only thing I had left of her was the note in my hand that no bunny ever would have written: *I can't do this. I'm sorry.*

She'd told me from the start. She doesn't date players. So what the fuck is she doing with Rux?

Was she lying? Because she sure looks comfy tucked beneath his arm.

My knuckles crack as fists form at my sides.

This is the kind of bullshit I'm supposed to be avoiding if I want a contract with Oregon. And shit, Allie isn't mine. She's just a chick who isn't as different as I thought she was.

I can walk out of here. Forget I saw her.

Hit another bar and find another girl.

Great plan.

Thing is, I'm not going anywhere.

Natalie

LIFE ISN'T FAIR.

After months of dodging out on plans and skipping games it killed me to skip, I join the guys for one stinking night to share a moment I'm honored to have been included in. *One night* and who the heck shows up but the *one player* I've been busting my backside to avoid since he was traded to the Slayers this summer.

Vaughn Vassar.

He's our second-line center, my brother's longest-standing rival, and the indiscretion I should have known would come back to bite me. Hard.

I gulp, hazarding another quick peek past the bulk of Rux's arm. My belly knots around the butterflies that have been launching like missiles since the guy walked in. It's definitely Vaughn. Even if I didn't know every face on my brother's team and most of the league really… for reasons I'd rather roll in hot coals than admit out loud, I would know his.

And in the eight months since I was this close to him, he hasn't changed. The dark waves of his hair still hang loose around a jaw that's heavy and square. But it's that hard edge screaming *doesn't play well with others*

4

chiseled into every line of his rugged face I recognize first. Maybe because I know exactly what happens when it softens… when those hard eyes crinkle at the corners and that slash of a mouth lifts, changing his whole face.

Like the rest of him, that contrast is hard to forget.

Hard not to think about when I'm not supposed to be thinking about him at all.

Cripes, why does he have to look so good with those dark jeans hugging around the mass of his solid thighs, the assortment of tats peeking out from beneath the deep vee of a T-shirt that's barely keeping up with the body it's been tasked with covering? And why when I've been surrounded by guys with this body type for most of my life—guys I wisely don't look twice at—is *this guy* so hard to ignore?

A breath shudders past my suddenly dry lips, and I lean back.

This is bad.

Honestly, the chances of him remembering a girl he spent a handful of hours with eight months ago are next to none. Most of the single guys I know in the league wouldn't. But Vaughn Vassar is a man too many people sell short and I'm not willing to risk being one of them.

Which is why I need to get out of here. And why I'm going to continue missing games and dodging out on plans with the team until Vaughn's contract is up and Chicago's most reluctant player moves on to a team he actually wants to play for.

Peering up at Rux, I give his shoulder a light slug.

"Hey, look, it was great seeing you guys, but I've got to take off."

He checks his watch and shakes the overlong mess of ginger he lovingly refers to as his *flow*. "You got practice or something?"

That would be a great excuse. Unfortunately the 12U girls hockey team I coach doesn't practice until Tuesday. "Not tonight. I'm just whipped."

With an understanding nod, he pulls me in to his giant chest, practically suffocating me in his armpit, before setting me back with a wink. "Good seeing you."

I steal one last glance at Vaughn. A waitress is taking his order, or maybe she's just chatting him up. I can hardly see past the rack she's got on offer about six inches in front of his nose. *Subtle.*

A twinge of jealousy blinks through me and it's definitely time to go.

I cut around our group and slip out the front into the cool October evening. The streetlights are on and there's a steady flow of traffic from either direction but no available cabs, so I order an Uber with less than a two-minute wait. The bar door opens behind me, and I turn toward the laughter, music and light spilling out onto the sidewalk—and freeze.

It's not him. It can't be.

He hadn't even gotten a beer yet.

He didn't see me. Wouldn't recognize me even if he had.

It's not—

My belly folds in on itself as eyes like granite lock with mine, and the one guy I was praying to avoid pulls the door closed behind him. "Thought you didn't date players?"

God, he's even hotter up close.

Arms crossed, he walks out to where I'm standing and props a massive shoulder against the streetlight.

The breath whooshes from my lungs, dragging his name behind in a shaky whisper. "Vaughn. I didn't think you'd remember me."

I'd been banking on it.

His brows lift, and his mouth—well, it's not exactly a smile he's offering so much as the absence of his scowl. "No?"

He looks like he's waiting for me to say something, but when I don't, the scowl returns, and he nods back to the bar. "So you and Meyers?"

What? "Rux?" God no. While most of Greg's team thinks of me as a little sister in some capacity or another, Rux has taken the back-up-brother thing to the next level. "We're friends. That's all."

He makes an indifferent sound like he couldn't care less, but the way he's looking at me says something different.

This I remember from Vancouver. This dizzying sense of there not being enough air when I had the full focus of his attention. This feeling of being caught in some kind of gravitational pull toward an object of greater mass. This borderline compulsion to reach out and touch. To run my fingers over the corded muscles of his forearm, trace the lines of black ink.

The door to the bar opens again, and I jump back, heart racing. It's just a couple girls huddled close as their thumbs fly over their phones. But it could have been my brother. Or Rux, or any one of the guys in there who would turn around and tell Greg who I was talking to, pretty much ensuring the start of World War III right here on the sidewalk in front of Belfast.

Clearing my throat, I shake my head. "So, it's umm… nice to see you again. But I'm uh… I need to get home."

There's another jump in that muscle beneath the scruff of his stubble, and even over the wind and roar of a passing bike, I'm pretty sure I just heard his molars grinding.

"Back to *Washington*? Yeah, quite the trip ahead of you."

My mouth opens, but I exhausted all my lies the last time we were together. Not that I can give him the truth. Vaughn's a better guy than most people give him credit for, but knowing how he feels about my brother… I'm not sure he could resist the temptation to shove our hookup in Greg's face.

A teal Prius pulls up to the curb and my breath rushes out in relief. "This is my ride," I say apologetically as I climb into the car. I know what I'm doing isn't fair, but it's the only way. "Take care."

Vaughn

TAKE CARE?

No fucking way that just happened.

But yeah, I'm standing on the street in front of Belfast, the spot Allie previously occupied, as empty as my bed the night she skipped out.

I ought to let her go. That's twice she's taken off on me. Twice I felt that weird fucking pull toward a girl I barely know, twice I was ready to break a few of my own rules, and twice she's left me standing wondering what the fuck just happened.

I don't need that shit, especially now. Except—

"Christ, Vassar, what happened to laying off Baxter?"

I turn to find my left-winger, Quinn O'Brian, behind me on the sidewalk, accusation pouring off him. I get it. Laying Baxter out at the beginning of the season was a fuck-up. One I've been paying for ever since. And if I fuck up again, it fucks things for our line. It fucks the team. And while I'm basically biding my time until Oregon can pick me up, *no fucking way* am I going to make *this team* a loser.

"Look, man, I just came out for a beer. I didn't know Baxter and half the team were here." Or Allie.

Is this a regular hangout?

"Yeah, and what about *her*?"

Her? Now he's got my full attention. "What about her? Who is she?"

"You don't know?" He shoots me a pissy glare I'm not in the mood for. "Natalie *Baxter*… She's Greg Baxter's little sister, and she's off limits, dipshit."

No. Fucking. Way.

Chapter 2

Natalie

*I*t's been an hour since I left the bar. An hour since Vaughn busted me trying to sneak out on him. *Again.* An hour since he let me go.

If he asks even one person about me, it's over. He'll know. And if he knows…

Biting my lip, I flip from the replay of last night's game to the local news and watch the ribbon at the bottom of the screen until I'm sure no one's reporting half the Slayers team arrested for brawling at Belfast bar.

Which means Greg doesn't know either. And for now, my secret is safe.

I change back to the game and watch Vaughn with a breakaway. He powers up the ice, outskating his competition, juking out Tampa Bay for a goal. The cameras cover him rounding for a fist bump with the team, but it's that moment before he reaches them that makes me shiver. He's totally in his own head and the intensity in his eyes takes my breath away.

That's not how he was looking at me tonight. But eight months ago… *man*, I don't want to think about how it was. What it felt like having his hands tightening in my hair and around my thigh. The way he looked at me when he groaned my name and—

Knock, knock, knock.

The remote flies out of my hands, clattering across the floor as I jerk up from the couch and stare at the front door like there's a poltergeist on the other side. Or worse… *my brother.*

He knows. It's the only reason he'd show up here without calling or texting first. So he can tell me that I just cost the team a top player midseason because I couldn't—

Knock, knock, knock.

Mouth dry and a sick feeling in my belly, I walk to the door.

I'm twenty-seven years old. Too old to be freaking out about Greg yelling at me, but I'm shaking like a leaf. Not because he'd ever lay a finger on me, or even because he's going to blow up… it's the disappointment I don't want to see. It's the letting him down and knowing that some selfish stupid act from eight months ago in freaking Vancouver might have implications for an entire team of guys I care about. For a team that means everything to my brother.

The knob is cool in my hand and I take a deep breath before bucking up and turning it.

I'm already apologizing when I open the door to six-foot-five, two hundred twenty-five pounds of bristling hockey player with one powerful arm braced at either side of the door. Only instead of meeting blue eyes that match mine, I'm confronted by the same steely stare I left back at Belfast.

"Vaughn."

"Just exactly what kind of game are you playing, *Natalie*?"

Vaughn

NO DENIAL. Not that I really expected one. O'Brian wasn't exactly uncertain. And then there was the way Allie—*Natalie* had been hanging around with the guys from the team. Baxter's guys. The way she knew me on sight in Vancouver. Like she'd known me for years… or maybe seen me going up against her brother from all the way back in high school.

I mutter a curse, and she bites her lip, looking away. Guilty.

"No game, Vaughn." A quiet sigh. "I just—I never

thought I'd see you again. I never in a million years thought you'd be playing here."

No. She just thought she'd use me as a quiet *fuck-you* to her brother.

Jesus, how did I not see this?

Yeah, I met her in another damn country after a game her brother wasn't even playing in. And I've never seen them together, but those blue eyes that haunted me for months... they're his too. Same with the hair. Dark brown with waves that are just a little wild.

Then there's the name.

To me she's Allie. But Baxter talks about *Natalie* at least once a week in the locker room.

Right about now, I'm wishing my go-to reaction for the past few months hasn't been to plug some noise-canceling headphones in the second the guy opens his trap. Maybe I would've learned something real about the chick who blinked out of my life as fast as she came in. Or maybe not, since I'd bet my left nut Greg fucking Baxter doesn't have the first fucking clue about Vancouver.

Natalie's looking me over, her brows pinched with concern as she studies my face, my hands.

Her breath shudders out, and that stiff posture eases a bit. "He doesn't know."

Ahh. Giving in to a humorless laugh, I hold up my knuckles for her examination.

"Nah, babe. He doesn't know."

Her visible relief pisses me off, because as much as

this is about who her brother is, it's *not about her fucking brother*. It's about her and me, and a night that ended too soon. It's about why she didn't say who she was and what she was thinking when she gave me that half-shy and half-determined look that got me harder than I've ever been in my life. Why she kissed me, pushing up to her toes and apologizing a second before those cherry ChapStick lips met mine in the softest, sweetest, hottest damn kiss of my life.

I shouldn't have a single fuck to give about this girl or her brother. I don't want to. But here I am practically twitching with the need to know. To understand.

It makes me nuts to think I could have been so wrong about her. About what was happening between us. Almost as nuts as it makes me to know fucking Baxter's got a claim on something else I thought was mine.

I've got my own history with the guy. We didn't go to the same high school or play on the same team, but even back then, the gloves came off often enough that the first interview I ever scored started with a question about the rivalry between us.

Fucker.

He got called up to the draft straight out of high school, while I was a year behind and played D-I at Notre Dame before making the NHL. And now with one year left on my contract, I get traded to the Slayers. To play second string to him.

Natalie stands in front of me, hands clenched

together as she worries that plump bottom lip between her teeth. Even now she looks so real, so authentic, I can't completely believe this is happening.

"I know you're mad—"

"Yeah, I'm fucking mad." She steps aside, and I walk into her place. It's a neat little townhouse in the Ranch Triangle neighborhood, on the small side for what her asshole brother ought to have her in. And not even close to enough security based on the fact that I just moseyed up to her front door.

"One—" I hold up my finger, ready to count off the reasons, "—I'm mad because the way you left was bullshit. Two, you lied to me. Three, you're fucking Baxter's sister. His *little* sister. Four, I'm mad because I can't even throw this shit in his face."

It would be epic. I can see him melting down in the locker room. Kicking his jersey like a total dipshit, eyes getting a little red and watery.

My kingdom for a single tear out of that douche.

Natalie's breath catches, and she takes a tentative step in my direction. So different from that first night in the bar when it seemed like she couldn't keep from stepping into my space again and again. Touching me when she talked, then realizing she was doing it and turning that sexy shade of pink before pulling her hand back and apologizing… only to do the very same thing again thirty seconds later.

She seemed so real.

Like there wasn't a contrived thing about her.

I don't get shit like that wrong. Except, maybe I did.

Those light blue eyes search mine. "You're not going to tell him?"

Shoving my hands in my pockets, I blow out a frustrated breath. "No. I'm not going to tell him."

"Why not?" she asks softly.

Because it would be giving him something I'd rather keep for myself. "Because I can't afford to start something with him."

Besides, as much of an asshole as I might be, I don't use women. Even women who used me.

Truth is, the biggest reason I'm pissed is because I thought what happened with us *was about us*. And now I've got to wonder if it was ever about me at all. Or if it was just about Baxter's little sister wanting to stick it to him by letting the guy he hates most in the league into her pants.

I don't want to think about that. Especially when I'm looking right at her and she looks like the same girl she was eight months ago with that crazy hot mix of bold and shy, sharp and soft, sweet and sexy. Christ.

His sister.

This explains why she neglected to give me her last name or her number. She knew going in she wasn't going to see me again. Would have been nice to get that memo before I spent half the night thinking maybe I'd found something different. Special.

My eyes narrow on her. Why would she do that?

Something else occurs to me. "Why haven't I seen you at any of the games? Anywhere?"

From the way O'Brian tells it, she's got surrogate-sister status with half the team, and that doesn't happen without being around a hell of a lot.

A wince. "I didn't want to risk crossing paths, just in case you happened to be… good with faces."

Good with faces. Like she was just some kind of filler for the night. Interchangeable with the usual bunnies. She's so far off base, it's not even funny. "Right."

I take another step into her place. Look around. The space is clean and neat. Blond wood floors with creamy walls. Simple sturdy-looking furniture that's a little big for the space but probably suits her fucking brother and friends. But it's the TV that suddenly snares my attention, because that's my face blown up to sixty-five inches.

Allie was watching *me*.

Brows inching up with the grin I don't bother to hide, I turn back to her. "Was I interrupting something?"

She follows the jut of my chin to the TV, and her cheeks flame red as she starts to sputter. "I was watching the game from last night—rewatching. The game. Not you." I wouldn't think it was possible, but her cheeks burn even brighter. "Okay. I watched you score a couple of times, but it's not like it was on some kind of loop to repeat. It was just a really nice play and and and—"

"And you're a fan," I supply, feeling a fuck-ton better about showing up over here after all.

Natalie nods, her breath whooshing out. "I'm a fan."

I wait a beat…

Her brows pinch, and her eyes flick from my mug on the big screen back to my knowing grin. "*Of the game*," she adds a little breathlessly. "I'm a fan of the game."

My grin spreads wider, because *this* is the girl from Vancouver.

"Yep. Got it." She's not *just* a fan of the game.

"Vaughn!" Oh yeah, there it is, the exasperated laugh she kept giving me that first night.

"*Vaughn*," I mimic, taking a step closer, because fuck if I can stop myself when her smile lights up like that.

"I was watching the *game*. I rewatch all the highlights." Her arms cross and her hip juts out. "So whatever you're hoping was going on here… forget it."

Wiping the smile from my face, I shrug. Wait a beat. And lean closer to her ear. "So you weren't watching my face, thinking about what it was like having it between—?"

Eyes scrunching shut, she clamps a hand over my mouth.

I'm pretty sure she doesn't mean to encourage me with all that shocked indignation. But even with just one night behind us… she ought to know better.

I'm standing close now. And when she meets my

eyes, her head tips back and she's *Allie*. She blinks, pulling her hand away.

This is the girl whose laugh and smile and soft, needy moans I can't stop thinking about. I went nuts when she took off like she did. No number. No idea how to get in touch with her.

But now here she is, those bright blue eyes locked with mine, her breath shallowing out as the seconds pass. As my fingers itch with the need to touch her.

She's right here.

I could do it. Reach out and slide my hand beneath those soft curls. Pull her in so her perfect little tits press into my chest. Take her mouth.

Slip into all that sweet and wet and—

But now I know who she is. And who she is, is why she left. Even before I was playing on her brother's team, we would have been looking at a total shitstorm if anyone found out she'd let me touch her. One I wouldn't have minded so much then, but with everything I've got at stake now, Natalie Baxter is a risk I can't afford to take.

I step back, crossing my arms over my chest. It doesn't feel like enough distance, but until I get past this initial shock, I'm not sure anything would be.

Maybe it's enough for Natalie though, because she smiles and shoves her hands into her pockets, shrugging her shoulders into a hunch.

She bites her lip and looks away. "So what do we do from here? I mean, now that you know?"

Now that I know her last name is Baxter and one wrong move means my career is fucked? And I thought she threw me off balance in Vancouver.

"For starters, you're going to start showing up for games and all the social shit you've been dodging to avoid me. You won't see me at most of it anyway, and even if you do, so what? I'm just another guy on the team and you're just another family member."

That pink bottom lip pulls free from the clasp of her teeth. It's soft and full, and I probably shouldn't be wondering if it tastes like the cherry ChapStick I'm betting she still keeps in her jeans pocket.

"Should we pretend we don't know each other? Maybe pretend we're meeting for the first time?"

Wiping a hand over my mouth, I laugh. "No way."

Natalie did a pretty bang-up job of omitting a few pertinent facts when we first met, but something tells me she's not quite the actress she'd need to be to fake never having met me before. Not after what we did.

"Nah. People will figure we've met somewhere along the line. No one is going to question it or be watching too closely."

"Makes sense."

I'm not sure what I thought I'd accomplish coming over here. It doesn't really feel like I got it, but it's time to go anyway. I walk to the door and when Natalie stops next to me, I turn to her. Let out a slow breath as I look her over. She's fucking Baxter's little sister and I've got a career about to go to the next level. Nothing is going to happen between us.

Still, that mouth. I can't help thinking about what it was like making it mine.

Natalie blinks up at me, nervous, sweet. "What?"

I don't have to answer. I could shake my head and walk out the door. But instead, I brush my thumb across the silky skin of her cheek. "You could have told me you were leaving."

"And then?" she asks, her voice unsteady.

"And then I would have kissed you goodbye just like this."

With my finger caught in the soft spot beneath her chin, I tip her face to mine and duck my head to press one last kiss to her mouth. Soft and slow, I hold that contact for a beat. Long enough to feel her quake beneath my kiss, for her hands to rest feather light against my chest… and to know without a doubt I shouldn't have let myself have another taste.

"See you around, Allie."

Chapter 3

Natalie

"*H*ello? Earth to Natalie," Helene Bomer sings, setting the roll of resistance bands she's carrying on the end of the counter where I've been updating the chart for my last physical therapy patient.

Glancing back at her, I make a face. "Sorry! What were you saying?"

"I was asking why you've been running your fingers over your mouth all day." Her arms come up and cross over her ample chest as she cocks her head and narrows her eyes. "But now I'm asking if you've been holding out on me, because there is definitely something going on here."

Sure enough, my fingers are tracing a path across my lips… and I've totally been holding out on her. It's been two days since my encounter with Vaughn, two days since the kiss I can't stop obsessing over, and two days since I've been able to look one of my oldest friends in the eyes.

But I can't keep this up. I need to talk to someone. I've just been too much of a chicken to do it.

Letting out a breath I didn't realize I'd been holding, I slump back and whisper, "It happened."

Soft brown eyes bug at me, and then she's got my hand towing me through the clinic to her favorite storage closet for gossip. I know better than to resist, and not just because she's a heck of a lot stronger than her five-foot-three stature suggests. I've known Helene since we played together in college. And now, just like then, this girl doesn't stop.

Pulling the closet door closed, she whirls around. "Does George know?"

She's talking about Georgia Bowen, goalie from our Wisconsin days and the only other person who knows what happened in Vancouver.

Scanning the shelves, I fiddle with a box of Kinesio Tape. "Not yet."

A couple swipes of her thumb and she props her phone against an orthopedic walking boot so we're both visible on one side and on the other we've got George with a wall of bikes behind her. She shoves a fall of red curls from her pixie cut out of her face.

Helene leans closer to the phone. "It happened."

Something heavy and metallic sounding clatters

against the ground from George's end, and she swipes the phone up so the background spins. When it stops, I can see she's in the back stairwell behind the shop. "You saw him? He knows?"

"He showed up at my door."

Helene gasps. "Does Greg know?"

"Vaughn says he won't say anything."

George huffs. "This is the guy who punched your brother in the face after one week of practicing together. I'm not seeing a lot of restraint there."

I shake my head. "Maybe not, but from what Rux says, Greg wasn't exactly a victim either. He just happens to have that whole hometown hero thing going for him, while Vaughn's new to the team and brings a reputation that isn't quite so polished."

"Whatever." George flips the straw on her water bottle and takes a drink. "I knew this guy was going to be a problem for you."

So the thing about George is, for as much as she loves hockey—playing it, watching it—she's not a fan of the pro players. Like, at all. I don't totally get it, but she won't get into the details.

And when I told her about Vancouver, I've never seen her look so worried. The only thing that put a smile on her face was when I admitted to not giving Vaughn my real name and then sneaking out while he was asleep. At which point, she jumped up on the couch with a whoop and grabbed my hand for a high-five I wasn't totally into.

Basically it's been eight months of her waiting for the other shoe to drop.

"I really don't think he'll talk. He's got too much to lose if they sit him with his contract running out." But also, for a reason I can't totally explain, I just don't think he would do it.

Both women start talking a mile a minute. Helene wants to know if the chemistry was still here. George wants to know who Vaughn thought he was showing up at my place like that. They both want more details about Vancouver and pretty soon I'm itching to escape.

Helene taps her lips. "I'm thinking we should meet at my house to discuss. I've got Doritos."

George offers up ice cream, but before they have a full buffet planned, I hold up a staying hand. "Sorry, girls. Home game against the Avalanche tonight, and I'm going with Julia."

And suddenly I'm thanking my lucky stars I'll be spending the game with my sports-obsessed sister-in-law. Because the last thing I'll have to worry about with her is getting grilled about my sex life.

"SO WHAT GIVES?" Julia asks, handing me a beer as she wiggles down in her seat, getting comfortable.

"Huh?" Pucks fire one after another, the guys lapping the sheet, stretching out, jostling each other with elbows and grins. Wagner Arena is unbelievable and Greg's seats are killer. I can't believe how long it's been since I came to a live game.

She looks me over. "You've been suspiciously absent lately."

It was bound to come up. "I know. Things have been nuts. I'm just glad it finally worked out today." Things have not been nuts and I'm turning out to be quite a little liar. It sours my stomach to think about all the people I've been telling fibs to, but this is one truth there is no way I can give up. Especially not to Julia, as I'm pretty sure spousal privilege ranks higher than sister-in-law secrets.

I take a long swallow and keep my eyes on the ice, waving to the guys who skate past, rapping the glass with their sticks when they see us. Watching the one man with the hard scowl who doesn't even look our way.

"You sure about that?" Her camera-perfect smile stretches and suddenly she looks a little dangerous. "Because I was thinking it might have more to do with a certain guy you don't want your brother to find out about."

My heart skitters to a stop. She can't know. *She can't.* Except she kind of knows everything. She knows *everyone.* Like not just around the NHL circles either. This woman could call up pretty much any pro player in the country just to chew the fat. And if they had a juicy bit of gossip, like say, someone saw Greg's little sister hooking up with his mortal enemy… it would take less than a nanosecond to get back to her.

Oh God, she *totally* knows.

"You can't tell him," I whisper, barely finding the air to push out the words.

"Ah-ha, I knew it!" she exclaims, springing up in her seat, sending her beer sloshing over the top of her arena cup. She takes a deep drink, bringing the level down, and beams at me. "Spill it, sister!"

Spill it? "Wait—what do you know?"

"Nothing, really," she confides easily, pinching her beer between her knees to adjust her blond ponytail through the back of her cap. "Just a hunch. I mean, the only time I've seen you miss a game before was because the girls you coach had one of their own. So I started wondering why you wouldn't be showing up." How could I forget, this woman has made her career by getting professional athletes to open up to her. What did I get myself into tonight? "I mean, to the best of my knowledge there wasn't a boyfriend. But what if there was? I know you've had some bad experiences with guys you date being kind of hung up on your brother, so it would make sense you wouldn't immediately start bringing him to games. First, so you could make sure he wasn't just in it for the tickets and, second, to make sure you didn't have big brother checking the poor guy into the boards for looking at his little sister. At least not while things are so new. Right?"

Breathing easier, I take a long swallow of my beer. A really long swallow.

She's off track. She doesn't know anything.

"So I get it, anyway. You want to spend time with this new guy, but not where Greg is going to catch wind of it. You're entitled to your private life." Julia flashes a wink at me. "Don't worry. I won't tell him."

At that I raise a disbelieving brow. "Really?"

"Okay, not unless he asks me. But seriously. He's not going to ask me. So dish. What's his name? Where did you meet? Does he like hockey or have you finally managed to find that one elusive unicorn who isn't into your favorite sport, but doesn't bore you to tears?"

Cutting a sidelong look at Julia, I realize there's no way I'm going to get out of here without telling her something. So I settle on the truth, but a stripped-down version that won't get anyone into hot water.

"Okay, there was a guy from a while back that sort of resurfaced lately, but it's not going anywhere. Heck, it didn't really go anywhere the first time either. But definitely not now."

"Definitely?" And great, why did I think Julia would let that go?

"And you're right, this isn't really something I want Greg to know about. For real." I tear my eyes away from where Vaughn is stretching out his legs, talking with O'Brian. He turns his head, looking out over the crowd, and my heart stalls... until he skips right past me. "He's not my type. At least not for anything long term."

Julia turns in her seat. "And in the *short term*?"

The short term was beyond any fantasy I could have conjured. It was so perfectly incredible, it physically hurt to walk away.

Reluctantly, my attention drifts back to Vaughn. Powerful and focused. That firm mouth and strong jaw. The eyes that look harder and colder than the ice beneath him.

Only I've seen them melt. I've seen them burn.

I remember what is was like having all that intensity focused on me. Those powerful muscles holding me like I weighed nothing. His mouth at my ear. "*Allie, I need to hear you come.*" Lower. "*I need to taste it.*"

I blink and suddenly it's there. Eye contact. Vaughn's impenetrable stare meeting mine like somehow he heard my thoughts.

My belly dips, hard, my breath shallowing out as my hand starts coming up in a wave before I think to stop it. Before I notice my brother cutting into my line of sight, wearing a goofy kind of confused expression as he looks back toward the pile of guys from his team. To where Vaughn's suddenly engaged with Doug Shore, one of the older guys on the team with a solid rep for playmaking, and a wife, Dee, who I adore almost as much as he does. Greg skates up to the glass, hits it with his gloved fist and points to the two of us, a wide grin stretched around his mouthguard.

My heart's beating so hard I wonder if Julia can feel it where our shoulders meet. But the look in her eyes as she watches Greg take another lap says she's not seeing anything but him.

The game starts, and the Slayers take an early lead in the first.

We talk about the players, the stats, and Rux's shot we both thought was going in. Between periods we grab a couple more beers and laugh about my mother's less-than-subtle hints to Julia and Greg about starting a family. But too soon, Julia circles back to the guy I don't want my brother to know about. And even though I try to keep my answers short and vague, I end up giving away more than I mean to.

"He's not even from Chicago. And trust me, he's probably less interested in anything happening between us again than I am."

Her lips purse as we watch center ice where a few fans have been pulled from the audience for a shootout to win five hundred bucks. "But he looked you up when he got here?"

I shake my head. "We bumped into each other. We made a little conversation, but nobody's getting the wrong idea."

"What, is he just in town for business?"

"Exactly," I say, thinking that'll be the end of an awkward conversation. But less than five minutes into the second she leans in.

"So you won't be seeing him again, huh?" When I

don't answer right away—because what can I say when I'm literally watching him right now—she gives me a smug smile. "I had a guy like that once, where I knew going in it didn't have a chance."

"Yeah, what happened?"

Taking a drink, she shrugs. "I married him."

The fact that I didn't see that coming is seriously disappointing, but before I can beat myself up too badly, Vaughn's off the bench, launching himself in the play. My skin starts to tingle as he picks up a pass from Popov and carries it down the ice.

O'Brian is open, and Vaughn fires between the legs of an opposing defenseman. A cut, a dodge, and when it comes back, he's in position to bury the puck with a one-timer that has the entire arena on their feet, jumping up and down with me.

I'm watching for that instant when he's in his own head, wanting to see it live and this close, but instead his eyes cut unerringly to mine and hold for the single beat that leaves my breath stalled in my throat before the guys are on him, knocking shoulders, bumping fists and slapping pads as he rounds the bench.

Julia cocks her head my way. "Damn, that guy is good. Too bad he's such a total asshole."

Chapter 4

Vaughn

"*J*esus, is that what you're doing here?" O'Brian scowls across the crowded bar to where Natalie is standing between her brother and Rux, talking a mile a minute. Her cheeks are pink, eyes bright, and her smile—damn, it lights up the whole room.

"Give me a break. My agent wants more of an effort to bond with the team." Technically, it's true. Travis Haybourn has been pushing me to make nice from the start. But if I hadn't overheard Baxter telling Rux that Julia and Natalie were meeting him at the Five Hole with the team after the game, no fucking way I'd be dicking around here dodging bunnies and ignoring nervous glances and too-loud whispers about my temper from *fans*.

"You sure about that, because the way you were looking at Baxter's sister…" O'Brian rubs a hand behind his neck and looks up at the ceiling like he might be praying. "Dude's going to tear my arms off if he finds out I told you where she lives."

Quinn O'Brian isn't a pussy. The guy's almost as tall as I am, a little leaner through the shoulders maybe, but I've seen what he can do to an opposing player who crosses him wrong. He doesn't want to get on Baxter's bad side, and he really doesn't like the position I've put him in. I get it.

"There's nothing to find out." This is the only player who gives me the time of day off the ice, so I don't want to make him sweat. "And even if there was, it's not coming back on you."

"You sure?"

I nod and change the subject. "Sweet win tonight, yeah?"

The guy relaxes some, propping an elbow on the repurposed air hockey high-top between us. "Hell, yeah it was." He takes a pull from his longneck and scans the crowd. Probably making a mental plan for who he's taking home. Guaranteed it's someone. "Surprised you got away from the press at all."

I grunt. Fucking media. One goal and two assists, but the first thing they wanted to know was what fucking Baxter thought of my game and whether the bad blood between us was impacting the team… If it bothered me that fans weren't embracing me, despite my play.

I'd have to care for it to bother me, and I learned long ago it pays not to.

We talk some more about the game. About a couple players we know from the other team. A call that didn't go our way and will be fodder for debate for the rest of the season. But all the while, I've got my eye across the room.

On the girl with the dark ponytail, black leggings, and Chucks. With the exception of the Slayers jersey with her brother's number on it, Natalie is looking all too much like the girl from that night in Vancouver.

I keep asking myself what it is about her that's got me so tied up, that had me searching the crowd from the time I walked out of the tunnel tonight until the second I spotted her next to Baxter's wife.

Like she can feel me watching, her eyes come up and meet mine. That smile I can't get enough of falters, making me feel like a shit for ruining something so sweet. I expect her to look away, to blush maybe, or try to pretend she didn't see me. But she doesn't. For a quiet beat, there's just her and me and this pull I can't explain.

O'Brian is talking about a trip he took to South America in the off-season last year, and I keep up my side of the conversation with the requisite grunts. But what I'm really thinking about is cutting through the crowd and pulling her away to a quiet corner… just like that first night.

I want to ask her what she was doing at the Canucks game all those months ago. I want to hear what she thought of the game tonight and know if she was watching me the way I watched her. I want her to give me one of those shy smiles that does shit to my insides I don't know how to handle. And then I want the smile that isn't so shy at all, the one I'm half hard just thinking about.

But none of that can happen, because she's standing next to her brother, and I'm trying to hold on to my career.

Fuck.

Rolling out my shoulder, I make a few noncommittal noises in O'Brian's direction before scanning back to Natalie… who's watching the motion of my arm with a look that's suddenly way less tentative and way, *way* less subtle. It's a look that could get both of us in trouble if anyone caught it… one I shouldn't encourage.

But *hell*.

It takes everything I've got not to lose the scowl in lieu of a shit-eating grin, but I manage. Just like I keep my focus off her directly as I switch arms to stretch out the other shoulder. Too slowly.

Thoroughly.

Natalie

OH. My. God. Vaughn's rolling out his shoulder and I'm pretty sure my panties are about to combust. I can't look away. I can't stop the hammering in my chest or the sudden dryness in my throat. I can't tear my eyes off of him as, bringing one hand behind his head, he talks with his teammate.

Cripes. It's a Tumblr-worthy stance that shows off the bulging muscles of his bicep, his powerful shoulders and broad chest beneath a custom suit shirt pulled so tight nothing is left to the imagination. Slowly his other hand comes up, rubbing a firm path across his pecs.

A sigh slips past my lips.

"Nat, what are you looking at?" Greg asks, cutting into my thoughts and making me choke.

I sputter to make something up, but he's already followed my stare.

No way. After all the games I've avoided and excuses I've made trying to protect my secret, my brother is going to bust me ogling Vaughn Vassar in this freaking bar? Only when I look back to where number forty-eight had been striking that criminally hot pose the moment before, my blood turns to ice. Vaughn's not stretching out his shoulders or talking to Quinn anymore. He's halfway across the bar on his way to *us*.

The air charges as my brother tenses at my left. At my right, Rux's head drops forward and he lets out a low groan. "What the fuck is with this guy?"

Greg cuts me a look. "Don't worry. I'll take care of it."

I'm definitely worried.

What is Vaughn doing coming over here?

Rux's big hand wraps around my elbow, gently tugging me back. Like he thinks somehow he's going to keep me out of whatever trouble's about to go down. I take a last look around one of my favorite bars, mentally calculating the damage about to happen. The authentic boards around the walls will be fine, but that scoreboard above the bar won't survive whichever two hundred-pound body hits it first. And the mini jumbotron replicas hung from the high ceilings… totally within the overhead arc of a barstool. And that's before the rest of the team joins the melee.

Goodbye, Five Hole.

Breath held, I brace for impact.

An impact that doesn't come. Because Vaughn barely even slows as he walks past us, jutting his chin at my brother and Rux with less than a glance for me. "Good game tonight."

I wait for the inevitable explosion, but the guys beside me are as shocked as I am. And then Vaughn is gone, disappearing into the crowd behind us. The breath rushes from my lungs, leaving me lightheaded as Greg shakes his head. "What the hell was that?"

"Fuck if I know." Rux pats my shoulder reassuringly. Like I can relax. It's over. The big bad monster is gone. "Probably just trying to stir shit up."

"Seriously?" I ask, looking from one to the other with enough disappointment in my tone they both cringe. "That's your takeaway from what just happened? The guy compliments your game and you think he's looking for a brawl?"

Greg's arms cross and Rux is suddenly interested in his phone.

Just then, Julia comes sashaying over. A couple long-necks in each hand. Her smile bright and wide. "What'd I miss?" she asks, pushing up to her toes to kiss Greg's stubborn jaw.

"Nothing." I clink my beer against all of theirs and take a long swallow.

Nothing except Vaughn Vassar being underestimated again and his quick thinking saving my butt.

IT'S ALMOST two a.m. and I've been home for fifteen minutes, but even the familiar lull of *NHL Tonight* isn't having its usual calming effect.

I'm reaching for the remote when there's a knock at my door. My heart stumbles, picking up a beat. It's him. Who else would it be?

Pushing up from the couch, I smooth my hands over my T-shirt, telling myself to be calm, that the jump in my pulse isn't because I'm relieved he's here. Telling myself that I wasn't waiting for him. Right, because I always watch TV this late when I have to be at work at seven.

I'm such a liar.

Vaughn's waiting on my front stoop when I open the door, his arms braced on the frame in a stance nearly identical to the one from the other night. Only the energy coming off him now is different. Still intense, but where last time he was agitated, defensive almost… tonight he's friendly. In a scowly, so-hot-it-hurts kind of way.

"Your brother give you any flak?" he asks, pushing off the frame and walking into my apartment before I can invite him. It ought to offend me, but I find myself smiling instead, the butterflies in my belly doing a nervous little dance.

"No one was paying attention to me or how I was acting around you," I say, following him down to the recessed living area. "I'm actually kind of embarrassed I thought they would."

Hands shoved in his pockets, he pulls his chin back with a frown. "Why's that?"

Really? "Umm, because in a room full of profes-sional hockey players, the last person anyone is going to notice is me." Heck, my own parents barely notice me in a room with just *one* player.

He makes a scoffing sound and drops onto my couch. "People notice you plenty." And oh man, he's doing that thing with his shoulder again and I'm a little nervous I might start to drool.

Swallow, Nat!

He rubs at his left pec with the heel of his hand, dragging it back in one of those mysteriously masculine moves potent enough to leave me breathless.

The corner of his mouth climbs perilously higher. "*I* notice you."

There's something in his tone—something taunting and amused—that has my eyes snapping up to meet his, and the whole shoulder-and-chest-porn business clicks. My mouth drops into a gape, and my cheeks start to flame. "You were doing it... *on purpose?*"

And then he's laughing, those granite-hard eyes crinkling at the corners. "Come on, can you really blame me? Having not just any beautiful woman's eyes on me but—"

"Greg Baxter's sister's?" I offer, maybe just to remind myself of who this man is and why I've always known I couldn't actually have him.

He shakes his head, any trace of laughter gone. "No, the girl who left me in a hotel room in Vancouver. The one who turned me inside out and then was gone so fast, all I had left was the memory of how sweet she tasted coming on my tongue."

On. His. Tongue.

Geez. I'm not sure whether I'm more embarrassed or turned on, but that clench between my legs and hitch in my breath says I might be lying again. Because I remember what it was like having his mouth on me too. The feel of that sexy mess of overlong hair sliding through my fingers and against my thighs. My back to the wall and one leg thrown over his shoulder. How he devoured me like he couldn't get enough and then how he slowly came to his feet and kissed me again. His tongue slicking against my own.

"Vaughn." I can barely hear my own voice. His eyes meet mine and hold for one awful moment when I realize that if he comes to me, if he says my name, it's over. I won't be able to resist. I won't walk away.

I won't stop to think about what's at stake for either of us.

But then, as if he hadn't just casually referenced one of the dirtiest, most intimate, incredible moments of my life, Vaughn leans forward and swipes my phone off the coffee table. Grumbling about how I ought to have a lock screen, he thumbs across the glass. "In case your brother manages to look past his own ego long enough to notice you staring at the one guy you shouldn't, you've got my number now." He pushes up from the couch and stretches again. No eye contact. No drool-worthy chest rubbing. Just the unconscious actions of a man whose body takes a relentless beating and needs some rest. It's still breathtaking to watch.

Crossing to me, he places the phone in my hand, his long fingers wrapping around so he's holding my hand for a beat as well. "Call if you need to."

Chapter 5

Vaughn

"Yeah, Travis, I know. I was there when they said it." My agent's pissed because of a soundbite from last night's postgame interview that's getting some traction on social media. The one where that dickhead Dixon Lannish essentially asked if it bothered me that half of Chicago thinks I'm an asshole.

It's bothering Travis, and it's bothering Coach, which means it's bothering me.

I push out the doors of the practice arena and head for the private lot out back, nodding at Bill, the guy working security, as I go. "What am I going to do about it, stand out front of the arena offering hugs to the fans as they walk in?"

This call is the last thing I need. I'm tense, itchy,

after seeing Natalie last night. I thought going to her place would take the edge off after hours of watching her get pulled into affectionate hugs and easy conversations with every other player at the Five Hole but me. And for the thirty seconds I was there it did. But then… *fuck.*

It would have been better not to go at all.

Better not to have her laugh with me. Better not to have been looking into her eyes while she reminded me of who she was—pissing me off so much, I ended up reminding her who she'd been to me. Better not to have touched her hand, even with that damn phone between us. Because then I was thinking about how soft her skin was… *everywhere*. I was thinking about what it was like having her laughing, squirming, over my shoulder as I carried her like a caveman down the hall in that hotel.

"Vassar, you listening to me?" Travis demands, and I can't even bite his head off and tell him of course I was, because once I started thinking about Natalie and all the places she's soft and tight and wet, and all the noises she made when I touched them—I didn't hear a word.

I stop at my black Escalade and dump my bag in the back. "Look, man, I'm not rocking the boat. I don't say shit about any of the players on or off the ice. I'm not fighting, and I won't." Because showing up at Baxter's little sister's house at two a.m. isn't going to happen again. I made sure she was okay. Gave her my number. And took whatever dirty thoughts I might have been harboring with me instead of putting them into action. "I'm keeping my nose clean and scoring goals."

"Keep that up, because Oregon fucking loves it. I was talking to the GM yesterday. He's got a hard-on for you, all right, but until we have a contract in hand, that could change at any time. Oregon likes your edge, but they're gonna like you a whole lot better if we get the fans behind you too."

Rubbing a hand over my face, I slide into the driver's seat and shut the door. "Yeah, just like that? Newsflash. These fans don't like me. They're pissed about the business with Golden Boy Baxter, and apparently, they're not going to forget anytime soon."

"They will. We've just got to give them something else to latch on to. Which is why we're changing the lineup on your charity work. Higher-profile stuff. I've got a consultant going through a list now looking for something to make you pop. I'll let you know where you're going when you come back from Philadelphia on Thursday."

"Yeah, fine. Set it up."

"Glad to hear you so amenable, because we've got another opportunity here I'd really like you to consider. And I think it would be gold for your image."

"What's that?" I ask, pulling out of my spot.

"Chelsey Channing's people reached out asking if you might be interested in some public appearances together."

My foot lands hard on the brake, the car coming to

a sharp stop. "What the fuck, *are you trying to get me arrested?* She's in high school!"

"She's twenty-two and actively trying to break away from her Disney teen sweetheart image while pursuing more mature film roles. The two of you could do each other some good, image-wise. You'd give her some edge and she'd be the girl that turned you around. Couple sappy posts on Insta about how you cried watching some romantic comedy and—"

"No," I say with a capital *fuck off*. Faking that I'm *not* into one chick is bad enough, no way am I going to fake that I *am* into another.

"Why, you got a girl?"

Allie's smile flashes through my mind and my jaw clenches. I need to get Natalie Baxter out of my fucking head. "No. No girl. Just not interested. Look, do whatever you want with the charity work. As much time as you can fill, fill it. But that's all."

Natalie

"DON'T THINK I don't know what you're doing," Helene says from where she is suddenly hovering over my shoulder.

I jump, banging my knee on the table and making the spoon fall out of my yogurt. I turn to scowl at her, but those crossed arms and jutted hip warn she's not having any of it.

"Don't give me that look. You know what you were doing."

Letting out a guilty sigh, I pick up my phone and make a show of tucking it into my back pocket. "I didn't text him."

"But you had his contact pulled up, and I saw your thumb twitching over the screen. What were you going to say? *Good game… I watched it four times last night and dreamt about it this morning… PS Thanks for the good time.*"

"I only watched it once." All the way through anyway. I might have spent a little more time on highlights, but as to dreaming about him? Well, that's been happening for eight months, so I'm not even going to address it. "And all I was going to text was a simple congrats on the win."

"And?" She knows me too well.

"And maybe a compliment on that play at the end of the second, because I've never seen anything like it and I know you haven't either."

"Mmhmm, it was nice." Helene nods, looking around the small clinic breakroom. "But I'm not going to fangirl him about it."

"That's not what I'm doing."

"Really, then what *are* you doing? Because I'm pretty sure you're the same girl who missed game after game just to make sure number forty-eight didn't see you in the stands or smile in your direction… and then get killed by your brother. Are you guys going to be friends now? Is that even what Vaughn wants?"

"No, I don't think he can afford the fallout any more than I can." And then there's the way he looked at me back in my apartment. Being friends isn't an option. And Helene's right that using his game as an excuse to text him would be a mistake too.

"Thanks for the intervention. It would have been stupid to text him. The only reason he gave me his number was in case Greg somehow found out. And he hasn't."

Helene drops into a chair by the window and opens her water. Jiggling her clog from the end of her foot, she blows out a long breath. "You know I love you. You're my girl. But Nat, let's say Greg could get past the whole archrival thing and suddenly he was all team Vassar."

That would never happen, but I wave her on.

"What do you want with this guy? You want to be Vassar's plus one? The WAG behind the player, packing up the house alone while he's on a flight to whatever city he's been traded to? Giving your one-week notice to whatever job you've settled into so you can follow him to his?"

For a lot of women, a tradeoff like that is one they'd be more than willing to make if they got to be the wife or girlfriend of an NHL player, but not me. And Helene knows it.

Growing up with Greg I've already lived that life.

I changed schools twice, once so we were close enough for him to play on a Tier 1 team in high school, and then when he got drafted, we moved again to be close enough to watch him play in Dallas. It didn't matter that I'd been selected to be captain of *my* team that next year or that I had friends or that I was happy. Greg was in the NHL. And that came first. Always.

But I promised myself it wouldn't always be that way. And once I hit college, I was free. For the first time, I didn't feel like the supporting cast member in my own life. I went to the school I wanted, got my degree, and then moved back to Chicago… *before* Greg was playing for the Slayers. Because it's where I wanted to be. Where I wanted to stay.

So yeah, not interested in a life dictated by the National Hockey League.

"I'm not talking about scoring WAG status." I've never even dated a hockey player before, but still. "There's just something about Vaughn that makes me want…"

She raises a neat brow and takes a drink. "What, Nat? What is it you want from this guy that's worth the fallout with your brother and probably something even worse for him?"

When she puts it that way, the answer is easy. "Nothing."

I might not want to marry Vaughn, but the guy means something to me. The last thing I want to do is be the cause of more trouble for him with this team… or worse yet the next.

Helene recaps her water and sets it beside her. "You know though, it would be okay if the answer was *something*. Or even *everything*. You know that, right?"

I don't. Because it wouldn't. Not really. I made myself a promise about the life I was going to have, and I'm not going to break it. "I just need to get through this season. I need to stay busy, and I need to put what happened behind me."

Chapter 6

Vaughn

*T*ravis gets shit done. And true to his word, he's got my every spare moment booked around the city. I've been to two pediatric hospital wards dropping off signed jerseys, hats and toys, a food drive, blanket drive, and an animal shelter where a photographer must have taken ten thousand pictures. Though if they got even one of me worth using, I'll be amazed.

I hate getting my picture taken and it shows. Fortunately, O'Brian was with me for the shelter and hammed it up for the camera, making baby faces at a dog that fit in the palm of his hand. And Popov did great at the hospital once the cameras started clicking.

But this, what I'm doing tonight, isn't something Travis set up. This isn't about turning my image around.

This is about kids being kids and making a sport that I've loved since I laced up my first pair of skates accessible to everyone. And best of all, there isn't any press.

It's already dark by the time I pull into the lot. There are more than a few spots up front, but I look for one toward the back just in case. I've got a gym bag with me instead of the usual beast that holds my gear, and when I walk into the rink lobby, my plain black Under Armour vest and beat-up Notre Dame ball cap ensure I don't attract much attention.

No one fumbles their phone trying to get a picture or post a sighting.

I walk into the smaller south rink and grin at the dozen pint-sized kids doing drills on the ice. A guy a few years older than me waves and skates over. I'm guessing this is Rick Scholtz, the parent coach I coordinated the visit with. And that would make the peanut decked out in pink and clinging to his pant leg his daughter, Eva.

She's got about four hundred sparkly hair clips attached to the silky ringlets spilling out of her helmet and a curious look in her soulful brown eyes.

Getting low, I smile and offer my hand. "Hi, sweetheart, I'm Vaughn. Would it be okay if I played some hockey with you guys tonight?"

She inches closer and nods, a tiny smile on her lips.

"You'll show me what to do?" I ask, and she giggles, burying her pretty little face in her dad's leg. Pushing to my feet, I shake Rick's hand.

"Hey, man, thanks for coming tonight." He's grinning from ear to ear, looking over his shoulder at the kids who've started taking notice of me now that their coach and hero is over here.

I shake my head. "Thanks for having me." After all the bullshit PR clouding what ought to just be something decent, it feels good to show up knowing this isn't about anything but the kids. Not having to worry about whether my smile is going to play with the public or keep cool when a photographer interrupts a kid to get a shot.

And maybe I needed a distraction from a certain brunette with dancing blue eyes and the sexiest smile I've ever seen. Being busy as fuck isn't doing it, but this —this just might.

I lace up my skates while Rick points out a couple of serious Slayers fans and chats about the slap shot the kid in the corner has. When I pull my jersey on and jump the boards—because you gotta jump the boards— I'm met with a series of awed gasps and a sea of eager faces.

"So, who's gonna show me the ropes tonight?"

An hour later I've given away all the jerseys and hats I brought to the rink, pulled a chain of kids around the ice a handful of times, shot pucks, practiced passing drills, and played Sharks and Minnows until Rick blew his whistle and everyone skated up into a neat line to thank me for playing with them. Each gives me a fist bump or hug and a smile that goes straight to the fucking heart.

After the last little hockey player is headed back to her mom, I turn around and nearly trip over my skates when I see *Allie*, sweaty, pink cheeked, and pretty as hell, standing in the rink doorway wearing a white and red Wisconsin jersey.

———

Natalie

MY OVARIES JUST EXPLODED.

I've spent the last fifteen minutes watching Vaughn Vassar—the man voted least friendly player in the league—playing Sharks and Minnows with a rink full of mite-level special-needs kids. Not for the cameras—there weren't any. And not out of some obligation—the full-on belly laughs and absolutely delighted gleam in his eyes leave no doubt about that.

Vaughn *loves* playing with these kids.

And any chance I had at putting this pesky crush behind me while he's still in town just went *poof*, taking whatever shot I had of cutting out of the rink before he saw me with it.

Hello, double take and slow, stretching smile. Oh geez, his mouth is something else. Coasting across the ice, he juts his chin at me with a taunt. "You following me, Baxter?"

I roll my eyes. "You wish."

"Hmm," he says, stepping off the ice.

I knew lingering was a mistake. Even now, I know I should leave, but instead I just stand there.

Vaughn straddles the bench and, eyes on mine, starts undoing his laces.

"You're pretty amazing with those kids." My heart is racing, my belly nervous. My words a little more breathless than I'd like them to be.

He gives his head a slow shake. "Those kids are pretty amazing, period. Fun to play with them today."

"It looked like it." I bite my lip, but then give in to the devil on my shoulder. "I don't think I've ever heard you shriek like that."

That smile. If the press got a hold of the smile I'm seeing right now, the city of Chicago and the rest of the world would fall in love with this man. His endorsements would skyrocket and the female population would flock to him in droves.

But today it's just me and the kids seeing the side of Vaughn he's so reluctant to share.

"What about you?" he asks. "You play in an adult league?"

Right, because while he looks hotter than sin, I'm sweaty and gross. Not fair.

"Sadly, my hockey-playing days are behind me."

His eyes skim down my body, landing on the knee currently screaming for some Advil. I'm wearing jeans, but I have the sense he's seeing the bare skin beneath.

"The surgery?"

I nod, my throat going dry with the memory of his mouth dropping feather-light kisses along the scar that runs the length of my knee and ended my college hockey career. The way he murmured "ouch" and promised to kiss it better. The feel of his stubble as he left the site of that old injury, kissing his way up the inside of my thigh, higher, harder, deeper… until I was gasping his name.

"Y-yes." And if that didn't sound guilty enough to give away where my head had just gone, I'm sure the flames licking at my cheeks will do it.

"You wouldn't believe how many times I thought about that scar," he says casually, putting his skates in his bag, like he's not talking about something he only saw because I was completely naked beneath him a few hours after we met. "It drove me nuts that I didn't get to ask you about it. I had a feeling it was sports related, but I didn't know you were a hockey player until I found out who you were." Then after a beat, he shakes his head. "The footage from that last game was intense. You were badass out there, but that collision was brutal."

"You looked me up?" I ask quietly, not sure I trust my own voice.

A shrug, but there's a darker tone to his cheekbones than there was a minute ago. "What, I'm not allowed to look someone up?"

He watched me play.

"Of course, you're allowed, it's just not many

people do." Why would they when my brother's worst day is better than my best. When there's a real star right beside me, unintentionally overshadowing almost every aspect of my life.

Coming to his feet, he swings his bag over his shoulder. "So if you aren't playing, what are you doing? Coaching?"

"Yep, 12U girls, and when schedules don't conflict like they did tonight, sometimes I help out with these guys too."

"That's awesome, Allie." The way Vaughn is looking at me has every cell in my body straining toward him on a molecular level, begging me to step closer, to give in to the pull that's been drawing me toward this man for longer than I'd like to think about.

Clearing my throat, I glance over to the rink door. "Well, I ought to get going. It was nice to see you."

"I'll walk you to your car." Stuffing a hand in his jeans pocket, he nods toward the back wall where there's an exit to the rear lot. "We could go out that way, so no one sees."

A shiver skates across my skin at the thought of being alone with him again. "Thanks, but I, umm, don't have a car. There's a bus out front that runs right by my house though, so I'm good."

Before my eyes, his features harden and the muscle in his jaw starts to bounce. "*Good* to get a ride from me, then. Great. Let's go."

I shouldn't agree. But the second Vaughn's hand

moves to the small of my back, I'm walking with him, my brain shut down to anything but the heat and tingle radiating out from that light touch.

The rear lot is well lit, but the handful of people at their cars are too busy loading and unloading gear to notice us. Vaughn lets me into the passenger side of his beast of a ride, his hand remaining at my lower back until I've stepped up into the seat.

Sliding into the driver's side, he cuts me a curious look and frowns. "What?"

"I think most people would be surprised by what a gentleman you are when no one's looking."

He huffs out a short laugh. "Yeah, that's me. Helping little old ladies cross the street and minding my language in polite company."

There's more to being a gentleman than limiting four-letter words. "I've actually seen you helping a little old lady. And she adored you for it."

In fact, I've seen him hold doors, assist with bags and offer his arm enough times that I have to wonder how none of it shows up in the press. All they ever seem to have are shots with Vaughn shooting death glares, bumping shoulders as he passes other players, and that "resting prick face" thing that I'm starting to suspect might be tied directly to knowing people are watching him. Because right now? It's nowhere to be seen. Right now, Vaughn's rugged features are relaxed, his jaw isn't set, and there's no dark shadow beneath his brows. He's so painfully handsome, I almost wish I could make myself look away.

But that's the nice thing about being in his car. No one can see me watching this closely. Except for Vaughn, and when he looks over at me for a moment, giving me one of those almost-smiles before turning his attention back to the road, everything feels *right*.

We talk about my coaching, and his away game against Arizona next week. I tell him about my job as a physical therapist and how I work with one of the girls I used to play with. He tells me about Quinn O'Brian's bet with Rux over the correct name of some iced coffee drink and how O'Brian ended up having to wear women's lingerie under his pads to a practice the week before. I'm laughing so hard it hurts, because this is what I had that night in Vancouver. This is the man I couldn't resist, even though it meant breaking every rule I had—at least for a few hours.

And when he pulls into a spot down the block from my place and cuts the engine, and my laughter quiets as he watches me with a look that tells me I'm not the only one thinking of that night, I wonder what would happen if I broke those rules just one more time.

He runs a hand over his mouth. "I need to know. Vancouver. What happened there?"

I'd figured it was only a matter of time before it came up. Had thought about how to answer. But now as he watches me, waiting for an explanation, I'm nervous to confess the truth.

"I used to watch you at my brother's tournaments. You were the only guy who wasn't either idolizing him or terrified of him. You were different, and I liked it." I take a breath, feeling the heat filling my cheeks and wondering if he can see it even in the dark. "But it wasn't just that. You were big and tough on the ice, but off... I remember watching you shoot pucks with the little kids between games, giving them tips and... I realized you were nice."

He rolls his eyes, letting out a low laugh. "Nice? Not a lot of people would have said that."

"I saw it, Vaughn. More often than not. And my crush kind of grew from there."

"It's weird to think that I could have met you back then."

I smile. "You actually did. Once." I lean in and drop my voice to a whisper. "You told me I had a killer slap shot."

This time he barks out his laugh and looks at me like he's searching for the memory. "So what happened then?"

"We moved to Dallas."

"Ahh."

"When we ran into each other in Vancouver..." Even now I feel that same skip in my heart. "I just wanted to talk to you. For a little bit. Find out who my high school crush turned out to be. And it seemed easier to be someone who wasn't Greg Baxter's sister."

Our eyes meet. "And?"

I swallow. "And then you turned out to be pretty great. And I thought, why not? Why not take this one night and forget about all the reasons I couldn't have you. Take one night to be the girl who could."

"You're killing me, Allie." Vaughn's focus drops to my mouth as he brushes his thumb across my lower lip. His eyes come up to meet mine, and the look in them has me forgetting about rules and *why*s and *why not*s completely. Time turns elastic, seeming to stretch and slow, pulling me closer with every breath. His. Mine. Then snapping back at the bark of a dog down the street.

Vaughn rubs his palm over his mouth and looks out over the street in front of us. "Come on, let's get you inside."

Chapter 7

Vaughn

$\mathcal{W}$aking up this morning was a bitch, but by the time I pull into the lot for morning skate, I'm ready to go. Physically, anyway. Mentally, I'm distracted as fuck.

It was a mistake following Natalie into her place last night. I told myself I wouldn't. The whole drive from the rink, the plan was to drop her and go. But for as much as I'm busting my ass to follow the rules, this girl has me breaking them on the regular.

Only to a point, though.

I mean, hell, I didn't pin her to her door the second I got inside. I didn't touch her at all. I didn't kiss her or fuck her or finger her or eat her or do any of the thousand-and-one dirty things that were firing through my mind from about the first minute I saw her standing there at the rink looking like every fantasy I've ever had rolled into one.

No, I was a model citizen. For two hours, I sat on the couch while she sat in her chair. She watched hockey highlights and I tried not to watch her. I tried not to think about how sexy she was in that old jersey or how hot it is that she was a player. And I tried even harder not to imagine what it would be like to have her in my lap instead of that chair…with neither one of us paying attention to the highlights as I teased my finger beneath her panties. In my mind, they're white cotton, like the hot-as-fuck pair she wore that night in Vancouver.

The ones I think about when I've got my hand wrapped around my dick, replaying the breathy, desperate sounds she made when she came.

Shit.

Yeah, I tried. But in the end, I just suffered through, talking my dick down every time he started getting ahead of me. And when I finally left, it was with a kiss on her forehead while she looked up at me with those big, blue, uncertain eyes. Because really, what was she going to say?

That she had fun hanging out and she hoped to do it again? We both knew I shouldn't have been there at all, and it definitely shouldn't happen again. Which sucks, because she's cool as hell and about the only thing in this city that makes me forget how much I wish I was somewhere else.

I shoulder through the doors into the locker room and half the guys are already here, joking around and giving each other the kind of shit Garcia used to give to me. There are a few nods as I walk through, but mostly they're watching Ruxton Meyers—

I stop and stare.

"What the hell is he doing?" I ask nobody in particular, watching his big fucking body springing into some invisible action, feet moving in place, arms out like he's barely maintaining his balance.

O'Brian walks past, nodding at the action with a grin. "Double-dutch."

"What?" But then I see it. Popov and Shore are at either end, arms moving like they're swinging jump ropes.

"Gotta give it to him, Rux has the moves."

Rux is crazy. And fine, the guy is all right. Or he would be if he wasn't hair-braiding besties with Baxter.

That ginger head comes up and he points to me. "You want next, man?"

I snort and wave him off.

But Baxter is up now, bouncing on the balls of his feet. And sure enough, he jumps into the ropes that aren't there, his feet syncing up with Rux's.

Jesus.

A handful of guys have their phones out recording, and one of them is talking about making Natalie's week when he sends it to her. Great, now I'm thinking about her again.

"Whoa, you okay, man?" O'Brian asks, adjusting his chest pads in the stall next to mine.

"Yeah, why?"

He shakes his head and sits back on the bench as I drop my gear. "For a minute there, you almost looked like you were smiling. I mean, no worries, that shit's good and gone, but wanted to make sure you were okay. No fever or recent body-snatching incidents."

"Ha-ha-ha. Fuck off."

"There he is. That's the guy we all know and give a wide berth to." He slaps my shoulder. "Enough dicking around, Vassar. Time to get on the ice."

Practice is brutal and intense and keeps my head where it should be. On hockey. But once it's over, I'm back to thinking about Natalie, keeping one ear open for her brother to start running his fucking mouth and spill something about her I don't know.

Like whether he's flying her out to the game tomorrow night. Or what her favorite cereal is. But all I get is that his wife is out of town and his parents came by to make sure he wasn't lonely and ruined some spank date he'd set up with Julia.

Shit like this is why I wear my headphones. But I can't keep them on for more than ten seconds before I dump them again and suffer through the monotony of my teammates' post-practice minutia.

Jesus, why can't I shake her? Six months from now I'm going to be half a country away and she's going to be here, coming to games wearing Baxter's number.

I need to get my focus on where I'm going, so once I'm done with tape and lunch with the team, I call up Garcia.

"If it isn't Chicago's sweetheart." He answers like it's been a day since I talked to him instead of a month. "Baby, you been missing my big stick?"

I snort, shaking my head. "You know it. Just not the one in your pants, thank fuck."

Jesse Garcia and I have been paired up since my rookie year. We clicked. He was my friend. And that was something rare for me. Right up until he got picked up by the new expansion team in Oregon. They wanted us both. It was part of the plan. My contract was coming up first, so they took him with the intent of me coming on board after this season.

The deal is as good as done. So long as I don't fuck it up.

"Things not gelling with O'Brian? You two looked pretty tight against the Predators."

That was a good game. "He's a solid player. And there are moments where it feels like something's there, that connection, you know. But it's not the same."

Not like it was with us, where I'd look for Garcia, and he'd already be where I wanted him to be, eyes on me, waiting for the pass I'd already be taking.

"It's one season, bro. Get through it and then get your ass up here."

Climbing into the Escalade, I close my eyes without starting the engine. "Yeah, I know."

"Haven't heard anything about you and Baxter mixing it up lately. You behaving?"

When I don't answer, he groans. "Come on, man. I'm not getting any fucking younger. I want the cup next year. And I need you to make it happen."

I get it. He's three years older than I am and while he isn't looking into retirement communities, it means it gets harder for most guys to come back from injuries and perform at the level we do without seeing some slowdown.

"I've been staying away from Baxter. But—" Shit, I don't want to tell him, but he's pretty much the only guy I can. "You remember the girl from Vancouver?"

Silence. Then deathly low, "If you fucked his wife, I'm catching the next flight and—"

"Jesus, no! What the hell, man?"

"Sorry, sorry. I know you're better than that." He takes a breath. "Okay, lay it on me. What about the girl from Vancouver?"

Look, I'm not a pussy. I'm a big guy with a don't-fuck-with-me attitude. Not much scares me, but when Garcia loses his shit— hell. This could get ugly.

Poking at the button that controls my mirror, I mumble, "She's his little sister."

There's a beat when I'm not sure he heard me, but then I wince as a string of angry Spanish fires through the line so loud I have to pull it away from my ear. I'm not fluent, but my guess is most of it's swearing, possibly with a few pleas to a higher deity thrown in. Definitely some threats.

When he finally comes up for air, I'm slumped in the driver's seat ready for the English translation.

Instead I get a disappointed sigh, and shit, that might even be worse. "Does he know?"

"No."

"You mean, *no, not yet.*" Another deep breath and I can practically see him shoving that hank of black hair from his face, head shaking as he mutters at the ceiling. "Because you know he's going to find out. The only question is whether it happens before or after your season is up."

He doesn't need to remind me what happens if it's before the season ends. Sleeping with the team captain's sister would definitely fall under the heading of confrontational bullshit. I'll get scratched from the lineup. I won't play. I won't even dress for games. Which could mean I don't get picked up by Oregon.

And Garcia wants me there.

"If Baxter hasn't found out yet, he's not going to. I'm not going to tell him, and you better believe Natalie doesn't want him to know." O'Brian knows there's something between us, just not exactly what. But I'm confident he'll keep his mouth shut, so no need to give Garcia something else to worry about.

"You believe that?" he asks hopefully.

"Yeah, man, I do."

A heavy sigh sounds through the line. "Okay. And

you're staying away from her, no eye contact, no conversation? If she walks into the room, you walk out?"

I rub the back of my neck, trying to figure out how to explain what I don't totally understand myself.

"Oh fuck, man," he sighs when I still haven't said anything. "Guess we had a good run. Hope you enjoyed your career while you had it."

Jesus. "Garcia, it's not like that. I talked to her a couple of times just to make sure we were on the same page. That she was okay." I mean, that was mostly what it was about. "But it's not like we're together."

She told me herself she could never sign up for the uncertainty and lack of control a relationship within the NHL meant. She wanted a life where she came before hockey. A life that she got to choose.

"Forget *together*. You sticking your dick in her or not?"

"Watch your fucking mouth," I growl, the threat in my tone unmistakable.

I'm answered with silence from Garcia and the slow popping of my molars grinding together as I suck a breath through my nose.

"You're still into her," he says, frustration coating his words. "Of course, you are. Six years and you never so much as ask a woman on an actual date. But Baxter's little sister gives you a couple of hours and she's all I hear about for a month."

"Doesn't matter. It's not in the cards for us and we both know it. And after the season, I'll be out of here."

"You hope."

I know. Whatever happens or doesn't with Oregon, Chicago is the last city I'd ever stay in.

Chapter 8

Vaughn

*I*t's been a week and a half since I saw Natalie, and yeah, sure, the road trip helped, but even when we touched down in Chicago, I held strong. No stopping by her place to check on how she was. It's none of my business. No asking if she'd seen the games—of course she has, and probably more than once—or what she thought of that play in the third against the Sharks. Nah, I went straight home like a good little NHL player and slept coma-deep until I had to get up for morning skate.

But now I'm edgy again. We've got a game tonight, but with all the hours in between, I ought to be grateful for the book drive scheduled this afternoon. But I can already feel the muscles along my spine ratcheting tight. It's not the event stressing me out. It's having a camera

73

trained on me for the two hours I'm scheduled to be there. I fucking hate it, but I'm going anyway because it's for a good cause.

I park in the back and it's a short walk to the square brick building where the door is being manned by a kid wearing a Slayers cap and an awed look in his eyes. I shake his hand and bite my tongue about the fact that he's wearing Baxter's jersey. I'm used to it by now. And who gives a shit. Once I get out to Oregon and I'm playing with Jesse again, this sea of number twelve jerseys will be nothing but a distant memory.

The kid walks me through a back hall, shooting anxious glances my way that make me feel like shit as we go. I like kids, and this one looks like he's going to piss himself.

"Erik, right?"

Now he really looks freaked, but he turns to face me. "Yes, sir?"

"Call me Vaughn. You play or just a fan?"

I know he's a player before he says it. "Player, sir."

It's the common ground we need and pretty soon he's running through his last game for me, telling me about the guys on the team, and the goalie he wished had moved up with them but went to play for the girls team instead… all in one breath. It's almost enough to distract me from the coming cameras and press, but as I get closer to the voices spilling out of the room ahead, I stop a second and rub the back of my neck. The kid stops too, looking between me and the end of the hall.

"You okay, Vaughn?"

"Yeah, man, fine. Just taking a minute before I go in." This is ridiculous. "Hey, you got a stick or something I can sign for you?"

He's like a blur darting off to wherever he's got his stuff, giving me a minute or two reprieve. If he moves that fast on the ice, this kid's got a future ahead of him. Laughter rises up from the end of the hall as Martin Wozniewicz makes a joke. But it's not my teammate's voice that has me pushing off the wall and edging closer. It's the softer, more melodic sound behind it. The one that slides down my spine and signals my limbs to move.

I stop at the doorway and watch Wozzy ruffle the dark curls falling around Natalie's smiling face. Swatting at his hand with another laugh, she turns around and stops dead when our eyes lock.

Wozzy follows her stare, brows digging deep as they land on me. "Vassar. Didn't know you'd be here today."

Yeah, and based on that half-stunned look, neither did Natalie.

He slings an arm over her shoulder, like he's going to protect her from me or something. "Hey, don't worry about this guy. He wouldn't be dumb enough to mess with you, but if you don't feel comfortable, I can take you home."

Christ. Does this dickweed seriously think I'd give her a hard time? Even without the history between us, I'm not a total ass. Just a guy who'd had enough of

Baxter's bullshit and was dumb enough to let him bait me into a punch.

Natalie laughs, stepping out from under his arm. "Give me a break, Martin. Vaughn's here for the book drive—doing something nice—same as you and me." She's talking to him, but her eyes are still locked with mine and damned if I can look away. "Thanks for coming today. We're happy to have you."

I want to ask her what she's doing here. How many places she volunteers her time. Whether she knows that for all the big-brothering treatment Wozniewicz is giving her, the guy's into her.

But Erik barrels back into the room, skidding to a stop between us with his stick held up in front of him, all eager and anxious. "Vaughn, I got it!" Then glancing around at Natalie and Wozzy, he adds, "I mean, if you still have time."

"Absolutely, man." I bend to one knee and sign it for him. He's beaming, and I clap him on the shoulder just as the camera crew and organizers come in.

"Oh, perfect timing. Let's get a shot of Mr. Vassar signing this young man's stick. Or maybe his shirt!" I'm not sure who the guy waving his people toward me is, but apparently he's in charge.

Erik's eyes shoot to mine and I shake my head. "No worries, kid, I won't sign your Baxter shirt. It'd probably burst into flames, right?" He laughs and stands a little closer to me. "But how about this, I'll sign one of mine and send it to you for your collection."

A blonde with no expression and lips pursed so tight I wonder if she needs a coffee stirrer to sip her drinks, moves in to start futzing with my hair and collar. It's torture, but as much as I don't like having this stranger's hands all over me, the fact that Natalie is here makes me feel like I just scored the winning goal.

Grinning wide, she holds out a hand for the kid. "Come on, Erik, you can give me your address and I'll make sure Vaughn gets it before he leaves."

The volume in the room goes up as directions are issued in rapid fire.

Natalie cuts me a glance over her shoulder that has me wanting to follow and lift heavy objects for her. Pull out chairs and open doors. Tease her into laughing just for me.

But she's fucking Baxter's little sister.

And while I gotta outweigh this little PA picking at me by more than a hundred pounds, I'm pretty sure she'd have my balls if I didn't let her finish. So I stay where I am while Natalie chats with Erik, asking about his team and what he thought of that play in the third against the Sharks two nights ago, because *it gave her chills*.

This girl is killing me.

And I'm pretty sure Erik's as much of a goner as I am by the time she's done with him. Poor kid.

I may be player-non-grata for the Slayers and city of Chicago in general, but I do my part for the drive, taking pictures and signing everything from hats, to phone cases, to jerseys made for a dog. Normally, I'd be one giant knot of strained muscles, but this time it's different.

She's here.

She's flashing me her mischievous smile while the PR guy coordinates shots and positions us for "candids" that pop.

She's watching me when no one is watching her.

And she's brightening every damn thing about today.

Wozniewicz took off about twenty minutes ago, but not until he pulled Natalie into a longer-than-necessary hug and told her to call him if I gave her any trouble.

What an ass.

When the last of the camera gear is packed up and the doors to the public are closed, and Natalie helps sort books and label boxes, I head out to my car and back it up to the walk. I tell myself not to think about hanging around while she finishes. Not to offer her a ride home again. *Shit.* That's the dead last place my mind needs to be going right now. We've got a game tonight, and demolishing the Bruins is the only thing I ought to be thinking about.

Rounding the car, I pop the trunk and pull out the dolly before stacking it with four boxes I've got to donate. When I get to the door, Natalie is the one waiting there, her eyes narrowed on me.

"What's this?"

"A few books I wanted to add."

"In addition to the check you wrote? The very *generous* check." The door swings closed behind us and her hand wraps around my wrist, butterfly light, but it stops me as effectively as if I'd walked into a brick wall. "And oh my God, are you blushing?"

No. No, I am not fucking blushing. It's hot in here and I spend my life on the ice. Or maybe I've got a touch of the plague.

"Big burly guys don't blush," I grumble, cutting a look over to where she's leaned up against the wall beside me, her eyes delighted, her smile breathtaking.

"So you're overexerted then, from all this heavy *rolling*?" It's a taunt, only the way she says it, sort of low and breathy, has my thoughts spiraling into a place I keep trying not to go to with her.

Too late. I'm staring at her mouth thinking about what it was like kissing her. Remembering how she bit my bottom lip, lightly, just enough to hold me where she wanted me while she licked it.

I'm thinking about her short nails at my shoulders and how her lips felt against my ear— "Okay, I'm blushing."

I need to stop looking at her jeans and thinking about how sweet it would be to get inside them, or to hear her breath hitch while I played with her. Right here. Against this wall.

I could have her coming against my hand in less than five minutes. I did last time.

Christ, my heart starts to jack and I'm about a

quarter second from sporting wood. "I ought to get these with the other donations."

Those neat white teeth sink into her bottom lip, and pretty soon I'm going to need more than this stack of boxes to keep her from seeing what it's doing to me.

"Yeah, of course. You've got a game tonight." She glances around and then asks, "Why wouldn't you have brought this stuff in while the PR guys were here? They would have eaten it up. I know you're trying to work on your image. This is just the kind of thing that would help. Same with that kid, Erik. He was beside himself when you signed his stick. But the minute the cameras came out you clammed up."

I could brush her off with some non-answer, but when she's looking up at me with those big blue eyes, I don't want to put a bunch of bullshit between us. I like that she's curious enough to ask me something. So I give her the truth. "Guess I just want to feel like some of what I do here is for me and for the charities I'm supporting. Not for my image."

"But if the reason you decided to donate all these books and tablets is because you wanted to make a difference, I don't see how letting someone take your picture could diminish that? I mean, you know what's in your heart, right?"

I stop the dolly next to a pile of boxes, and Natalie immediately grabs the top one off the stack. I grab it back, laughing. "Christ, first with the blushing and now you want to help me carry my boxes? You trying to drive my ego into the ground here?"

"Something tells me that thing wouldn't stay down for long. But no, just helping."

I shake my head because now she's got another box. I set the first one aside and reach for the one in her hands. Our fingers touch and it's like someone plugged me into a socket. I feel the heat from that accidental touch like lightning through my nervous system, like a fucking current beneath my skin. But a good one.

Her eyes cut to mine, going wide before darting away.

And now I'm not the only one with pink cheeks.

Chapter 9

Vaughn

*H*er fingers slide free of mine. I set the box aside as she takes a few steps away and then turns back to meet my eyes.

"Do you ever wonder what it would be like if things were different?" She gives me a small shrug. "If we could be friends?"

"Friends?" I'd like to be the kind of good guy where that would be enough, but all it takes is looking at her to know it wouldn't.

Wetting her lips with the tip of her tongue, she walks through the piles of boxes. Her fingers trail across cardboard before she stops at a foldout table set up with a laptop and the clipboards the volunteers were using during the event. Leaning back on it, she looks up at me, her eyes soft.

"That would be something, huh? If we were friends. Can you imagine it?"

There's something about the way she says it. A vulnerability that won't allow me to let her down. So even though I know I'd want more, I take a couple steps in her direction and nod. "Sure, I can. I'd be lucky to have a friend like you." I jut my chin at her. "You could give me some pointers on my slap shot."

Christ, that smile. But then it's gone, and it feels like the sun just set for the last time. "Allie—"

"What if it didn't have to be such a big deal, Vaughn?" Her eyes search mine. "I mean, would it *really* be that big of a deal?"

It would. No one would believe that a friendship with Natalie Baxter was about anything but me fucking with her brother. Which means a friendship with her would cost me my season and that could cost me my career. She knows it. This girl understands the world I live in almost better than I do. But for whatever reason, in this moment, the reality of that world isn't where she wants to be. And so I cross my arms and listen.

"We've bumped into each other enough times that it makes sense we'd say hello after the games, right? Have a few private jokes between us about that time at the book drive," she says, a soft plea in her too-blue eyes.

A plea I can't resist. "And at the rink." The memory of finding her there, sweaty and pink-cheeked, so fucking pretty, pulls at the corner of my mouth. "All the kids."

84

She nods, pleased that I'm playing along. "So we talk a little."

"But not too much." I step up to the table, leaning into it beside her. "Not too long."

"Because Greg will hate it, but if it's just a minute here and there, what's he really going to say, right?"

Baxter? He'll have plenty to say and my guess is that it wouldn't be with words. It would be with his fists.

But that's not what I tell her, because the smile this game of *what if* is earning me is too sweet to give up. And maybe I want to see the kind of ending Natalie would write us, even if it's only within this bubble in the back room of the book drive. So I take another step into the shared fantasy. "Nothing. He wouldn't say anything. Because we're just talking about volunteering."

Her voice softens. "And little by little our talks last longer."

"And it's no big deal, because it would be a gradual thing."

She nods. "*Slow.*"

"And then when I leave?" Because I will. I have to. *I want to.*

"You'll have a few people meet you at Belfast for a goodbye drink. And by then everyone will know we're friends, so it won't be any big deal at all when I give you a hug goodbye."

I can practically feel her chest pressed against mine,

her slim frame filling my arms. "For a minute. And then I'll let you go."

She nods once, some of the light in her eyes dimming as she stares at the floor. It ought to be the end of the story except I don't want it to be. Turning into her, I reach for her, tipping her face toward mine. "And then maybe one day, because we're friends, I'd fly you out to one of my games."

"In Oregon?"

"Yeah." I shouldn't be touching her, but her skin is so soft I can't make myself stop. "And this time, you'll be wearing a jersey with my name on it." Christ, just the idea of having her wrapped up in my number sparks something in my chest that shouldn't be there. Something hot and possessive.

"I'd cheer for you and you'd knock the glass as you skated past."

"After the win—" because if she was there, there's no fucking way we wouldn't win, "—I'd take you to dinner so we could catch up."

"We'd talk. For as long as we liked, because it wouldn't matter anymore if anyone saw."

"I'd make you laugh so you were smiling just for me."

"And after, you'd take me back to my hotel," she whispers.

I should. But even in the context of this friendly fantasy that's more than a year off and will never actually happen, I know that's not the way it would go.

Giving in to the pull inside me, the one I feel every time this woman is within sight, I plant one hand on the table beside her hip. I'm crowding her. Standing so close I can smell the faint scent of her shampoo. Her pupils are blown wide and I can hear the change in her breathing. See the flush across her chest and neck.

"That's not what I'd do," I say, my voice gravelly low.

Her lips part and then she asks quietly, "Why not?"

The shyness that gets to me in ways nothing and no one else can is there, goading me on. Making me take it further.

"Because after dinner, I'd take your hand to help you up. And even though I'm trying to be good, even though I know better—" my fingers slide around the back of her neck, weaving into her dark curls, "—something happens when we touch."

"What?" she asks, breathless and beautiful.

"You look at me like you are right now." I bow my head toward hers. "And all the good intentions in the world aren't enough to stop me."

"Vaughn…"

But whatever she's about to say next gets lost in the brush of my mouth against hers. This wasn't part of the plan. It's a mistake and we both know it, but when her hand moves to my chest, her fingers closing in the fabric, all I can think is *this is right*.

I kiss her again, groaning as I sink into the softness of her mouth, tasting the quake of her breath and the give of her lips opening beneath mine. The tentative stroke of her tongue against mine. Shy and bold.

Perfect.

My arm tightens around her waist, gathering her closer until she's pressing into me with all those sweet curves and light touches. Clinging and holding. She feels so good.

"*Allie*," I rasp against the skin along her neck, breathing her in while I try to hold myself back.

We're not alone. Not really.

She tugs me closer, and the part of me that's been waiting for her since Vancouver snaps. I'm all over her. My hands are in her hair, on her ass, and—when I hear that soft whimper that matches the one that's been haunting my dreams for the better part of a year—pulling at the back of her knee so it's hitched against my side and I can feel where she's warm and soft against my thigh.

More. I angle her head back to deepen my kiss, thrusting with my tongue the way I want to be with my dick. And holy hell, the way she moans around me has my hands fisting in her jeans as her hips rock into mine.

Snapshots of every fuckable surface in the room flash through my mind. The table, wall, and door… The hip-high stack of boxes to my left—

A clatter sounds from the hall, and Natalie jerks back with a yelp.

I reach for her hand, not caring who's there, if it's her brother or my coach or fucking TMZ. But she skirts away, checking her clothes and touching her mouth with shaking hands like she's trying to erase the evidence of our kiss.

"Hey, it's okay."

She nods tightly, eyes shooting to the empty doorway where there's more rustling from the hall and some muffled cursing. "I don't think anyone saw us." She takes another step back. "I shouldn't have done that. It was a mistake."

Whoa. Shaking my head, I cut another glance at the door and, stepping closer, lower my voice. "The hell it was. Allie, we could—"

A guy in a red volunteer shirt steps through the doorway, stops, and pales.

"Oh shi— Umm, Mr. Vassar, I didn't realize you were still here," he says, juggling a box that looks like he took it bowling.

"Vaughn had a couple of donations he forgot to bring in earlier," Natalie says too quickly, putting a few more feet between us. But the guy hasn't taken his eyes off me.

Forcing my feet to move, I meet him and take the box before he dumps it again.

"Th-thanks." He sounds like he's afraid I'm going to pull his shirt over his head and sock him. "You know you can take off, right?"

I don't want to take off. I want to take Natalie in my arms and bury my face in her hair while she breathes against my neck. I want to carry her heavy boxes and then give her a ride back to my place so I can lose myself in her body, so deep and so good, she forgets all the reasons this is a mistake. We both do.

Natalie shoves her hands into the back pockets of her jeans and doesn't quite meet my eyes. "Yeah, you've got a game tonight. You ought to get some sleep… or whatever you do." Then, like she knows I'm going to try to get her to come with me, she directs her next words to the guy. "I've got some paperwork to wrap up, you want to make sure Vaughn gets out okay?"

He looks like he's going to swallow his tongue, so I hold up a hand. "I know my way. Nice job today. Thanks for your help, Natalie." I wait until her eyes meet mine. "See you after the game."

Chapter 10

Natalie

My stomach is in knots, and it's not because we're 2-2 with a minute left in the third and Boston has control of the puck. No, it's the man ready to vault into the action that has me all tied up.

"See you after the game."

Not maybe he'll see me. Just that hard, level stare that spoke louder than his words.

God, what was I thinking kissing him like that?

I know better. For myself and for him. I've spent half my life in the shadow of a star that burned too bright for even my own parents to notice me behind it. Half my life finding out that too many friends weren't really *my* friends at all, just fans looking for an all-access pass to my brother. Half my life being forced to give up the things that mattered most to me for the sake of Greg's skyrocketing hockey career.

When it comes to the rest of my life, I'm going to be more than a supporting character. That's why I've never been interested in an NHL player… well, except for Vaughn. But even with him, it wasn't like I wanted to *date* him. I never wanted to score a permanent position on the sidelines of his life. I just wanted—I wanted to know what it was like to talk to the guy who'd caught my interest back when he was still a boy, and then I wanted to know what it felt like to give in to the only attraction that has ever completely overwhelmed me.

But just once.

After that I was supposed to *want* to walk away. But walking away that night in Vancouver was brutal. And the only way I managed it at all was counting the ways I was never going to let anyone's hockey career make me take a backseat in my life again. I've been doing it since the trade at the start of the season. And today I've been grasping to hold on to the most brutal sacrifices made on the altar of Greg's career because the second I stop, I'm thinking about Vaughn.

About the way he plays with little kids and how his own generosity embarrasses him. I'm thinking about the rare smile I'm fairly certain I've seen more than everyone else in this city combined, and how it makes me melt every time I get a peek at it. I'm thinking about the way he looked at me before he kissed me today and even more… the way he looked at me after. I'm thinking about the feel of those powerful arms closing around me and how I can't remember anything in my life feeling as right as being within them.

Enough. I'm smarter than this.

Eyes on the game.

Greg takes a hit the refs miss, and the crowd erupts around me, screaming at the officials as he skates toward the bench. But what I'm focused on is Vaughn blasting onto the ice like a force of nature, cutting around one player and then, lightning fast, changing direction to intercept a pass. The puck is his, and with three Bruins players right on him, he moves it between his skates and then theirs, passes to O'Brian who gets it to Diesel. Back to Vaughn. My heart stops and I'm out of my seat as Chicago's least popular player charges into an opening a sliver wide and, with fifteen seconds left on the clock, turns an impossible play into a Slayers win.

The fans go wild, pounding the glass to cheer as Vaughn's met with a clobbering hug from O'Brian and Diesel as they pass the bench in a growing cluster of celebration.

And all the while, he's watching me.

See you after the game…

It's in his eyes. It's in that cocky half smile he so seldom lets off the leash. It's burning low in my belly, making me ache. Tingling over my still-sensitive lips.

Everyone is talking about Vaughn as the stadium clears out. There's something different in the way they say his name tonight. Same is true when we get to the Five Hole.

Vaughn's not standing at the far end of the bar, warding off bunnies while he talks to one of the few guys on the team he manages to get along with. No, he's surrounded by seven teammates, all laughing and clapping his shoulders and treating him like—heck, like he's part of the team and not just the jerk who took a swing at their captain a week into the season.

It looks like he's doing exactly what his agent told him he needed to. He's getting his team behind him and reminding Oregon why they want him.

Vaughn's eyes come up, unerringly finding mine with that shiver-and-burn intensity. My mouth goes dry and, for a beat, I can't move. I can't do anything but wish things were different.

I take a steadying breath and give him an apologetic smile I know he understands from the way his brows dig together, and then I leave before either of us does something stupid.

When I get home, I kick my Chucks into the corner by the closet and look around my empty apartment feeling at loose ends. I don't trust myself with the replay of the game I just watched. I can't handle seeing Vaughn Vassar looking at me like that again tonight. Not without risking things neither of us ought to risk.

Closing my eyes, I slowly lower myself to sit at the stepdown to the living area and try to focus on all the reasons leaving the bar was the right thing to do. Telling myself that kiss from this afternoon was a mistake, no matter how good it felt.

So good.

I could be back at the bar in—

Knock, knock, knock.

Sucking in a startled breath, I push to my feet. My heart speeds as that restless feeling in my belly turns into a kind of instinctual pull that draws me to the door.

I don't have to check to know this isn't my brother.

It's not George looking to chat, or Helene showing up with snacks and office gossip.

Not tonight.

My fingers tingle as I reach for the knob, my heart races, and my mind empties of all the reasons this is a mistake. Of everything except the relief surging through my veins as I swing the door open. Vaughn is braced against the frame again. He's lost the suit jacket, and his big arms are flexed and straining as he barely holds himself back.

"I shouldn't be here," he says, the words gravel rough and rubbing against me in ways that only make me want to hear more. "I don't even have a fucking excuse to check on you."

"But you came anyway," I whisper, drinking him in.

"I came anyway."

The muscle in his jaw jumps as his silver eyes swirl with an intensity that matches the energy coming off him in waves. I shouldn't be reaching for him, but I don't think I could stop if I tried. I want this. I want him. My fingers curl into the gap between the buttons of his dress shirt and I tug.

There's a beat of resistance when he pulls back and our eyes connect—and then he's launching forward on a growl so savagely possessive, I feel it through the deepest part of me. That big arm I couldn't stop staring at sweeps around me as his mouth crashes against mine in a feral kiss. This isn't tender or tentative. It's desperate and hungry and has me half climbing his body before my shoulders hit the door he just swung shut with his foot.

Hands roaming over my thighs and ass, he alternates between gentle and desperate, stroking one second and gripping the next. Making me groan around the thrust of his tongue. Making me rock into that thick, steely ridge lodged between us.

"Allie, tell me this isn't a mistake."

I need more of his mouth, more of his kiss. More of his huge chest pressing hot and hard against my own so I can't feel anything but him. "It's not a mistake."

It's critical. Necessary.

It's my first full breath in weeks, months. "We just— we just need to get it out of our system. That's all."

His nostrils flare, and his eyes burn over me as his hand tightens in my hair. "I don't think—" But instead of finishing whatever he was going to say, he blows out a harsh breath and gives me a single nod.

And then I have it, the crush of his kiss. So potent, I feel it hot and pulsing, straight through my center. Opening further, I moan around the taste of him filling my mouth and stroking firm against my tongue.

One hand slides up my waist, my ribs, and then to the underside of my breast. He kneads it with a rough touch that sends spasms between my legs.

"More," I gasp, trembling as I squirm, trying to get to the buttons of his shirt, then trying to pull it free of his suit pants as we rock together, frantic for more of the sweet friction that's making me insane.

Oh God, *the contact.*

His huge hands grip my thighs and ass. The room spins around me and suddenly he's walking us back through my too-small apartment to my bedroom, kissing me all the while, driving me crazy.

"Christ, baby, if we only get one night, I want to spend it inside of you."

"Yes." I need him. Now. "Clothes."

I've been working on his shirt since he crossed the threshold to my place and I've barely gotten three buttons undone. But in less than a breath, Vaughn takes a handful of my shirt and, pulling it overhead, tosses it aside. He looks down at my sparse chest and the plain gray cotton bra even more bland than the one I was wearing in Vancouver and groans like it's the sexiest thing he's ever seen in his life.

And then he's got it unclasped and following the way of my shirt. The cool air kisses my straining nipples before Vaughn covers one and then the other with the wet heat of his mouth. He could tease me like this forever, but we've reached my bed.

I bounce back on the mattress, and a second later, he's whipping my jeans and panties off my legs. He jerks his shirt off in one pull and loses the belt, pants, and boxer briefs just as fast.

My belly does one of those needy little flips, and my mouth goes dry.

Because, just wow. His body. It's a masterpiece.

Broad and powerful. More beautiful than I'd allowed myself to remember.

Packed with heavily layered muscles that flex and shift, ball and stretch as he follows me onto the bed. His skin is a shade warmer than mine and inked up one arm and across his chest. A dusting of dark hair swirls around his nipples, bisecting the hard slabs of his abdominal muscles and trailing lower to where his cock juts thick and long.

I've dreamed about this body.

Moving between my legs, he pulls my knee up his side.

It's been almost a year since we did this last. Since he spent hours teasing me, making me come before finally, finally sinking inside me in one deep, smooth thrust. I can't wait that long again. I can't wait another second.

Cupping his rugged jaw, I tip my hips in invitation. "Inside me."

Staring into my eyes, he nods. Frowns and mutters a

curse with a shake of his head as he rocks back on his knees. "Condom, baby."

Right. Condom. I'm on the pill, but that's not the sort of thing I should forget. Ever. But cripes, protection hadn't even crossed my mind. It ought to be enough to snap me out of this haze, to catapult me back to reality, but I'm too far gone. "Hurry."

Producing a square foil package I didn't notice before, he rolls it down his thick cock and then leans back over me. "I don't want to hurt you."

I whimper in protest. He can hurt me. He can do anything, so long as it eases this emptiness.

But then he's reaching between us to run his fingers through me. One slick stroke and his eyes close in what looks like something between pleasure and pain.

"Your pussy's so wet for me."

He works a blunt finger inside me, pumping slowly in and out as I gasp and writhe. I'm dying for him.

"So tight." Adding another finger to the first, he stretches and twists. "I'm about to lose it just from touching you."

I'm panting, clenching around him, halfway there already. My hands are on his chest, my thumbs playing with his nipples and the deep grooves between his muscles. Lower. I graze his shaft.

The noise he makes is guttural, unintelligible, and emanates from somewhere deep in his chest. Our fingers brush as he takes his cock in hand and guides the thick head through my folds until he's notched at my opening.

Our eyes lock.

This is it.

What I've been telling myself I didn't need, shouldn't miss, and can somehow live without.

What I've been lying about for months. "Vaughn, please."

His hips rock forward, and he's pushing inside me, stretching me wide, wider. Sinking deeper. My breath is lost, my fingers gripping the unyielding slope of his shoulders.

"*Allie*," he rumbles through gritted teeth. "I've thought about this. So many times. About the feel of you around me." There's so much of him, I feel full already, but he keeps pushing, retreating and then giving me more. "The taste of you coming on my tongue."

"*Vaughn!*"

"Fuck... you saying my name just like that. *I've dreamed about it.*"

And then he's as deep as he can go, holding against that straining boundary as my body grips and clings, grasping at him with needy clutches.

Stormy eyes search mine and he runs a gentle touch across my jaw. "You okay?"

"Yes." So much more than that.

He starts to move, dragging his heavy shaft out in a slow stroke before sliding back in to nudge that spot so deep inside me, it steals my breath, and then retreating to do it again and again and again.

I'm chanting his name, rushing toward the place only he's taken me before. My knees hitch higher and his hand slides over my leg in a caress as he holds himself above me with one arm.

"Fuck, Allie, you feel so good. Too good." He rocks into me again, hitting that spot a little harder, making me spasm around him. "I want to make it last." *Harder still.* "But I can't wait." Oh God, *that spot*! "I've got to make you come."

"Yes... close... please," I gasp, hands everywhere, tumbling toward release.

"Come for me, baby," he growls, gripping my ass in one huge hand and tipping my hips into his.

And I'm there.

Falling over the edge.

Coming around Vaughn's hard thrusts.

Crying out his name as pleasure and relief fist within me, gripping and releasing in wave after wave, until I fall limp and Vaughn goes tense above me. Another thrust and he holds himself deep inside, pulsing hot as he follows me over.

Sliding my knees up his sides, I lock my ankles around his hips and hold him to me, just for a minute. I'm not ready for this to end and I don't want to have to face what's coming next. But all too soon I am.

"Give me a second to take care of this." He's halfway to the bathroom when he stops and looks back at me with a hitch at the corner of his mouth. "Don't go anywhere."

"My place." I laugh. "Where am I going to go?"

"Don't make me find out."

A minute passes and he's back. Wearing only the marks of my hands on his skin, he sits beside me on the edge of the bed and traces his thumb along the line of my ribs, down and around my navel.

"Regrets?"

It's easier to follow the light touch coasting across my skin than meet his eyes. "No," I answer quietly. Honestly.

What just happened wasn't a mistake. It was perfect. All the things I wish I could find with someone who wouldn't make me break every promise I've ever made to myself. "But…"

He nods. "But you still don't date hockey players and I've still got a career on the line. I get it. I do." He stands, and my heart starts to ache. But instead of reaching for his clothes and leaving, he reaches for the edge of the sheets and gestures for me to get in.

And then he climbs in behind me. "But I'm going to hold you tonight."

And that's what he does.

Chapter 11

Vaughn

*I*t's barely after four. I ought to be dead to this world, but I'm wide awake, lying in Allie's too-small bed, breathing in the scent of her hair as it spills across my chest. Just one more minute and I'll untangle our legs and slip out from beneath her. Drop a kiss on her cheek and get out of her place before anyone catches me doing it.

One more minute. Because this—Allie tucked into my side, her soft breath washing over my skin, her arm draped across my stomach—this is what I thought I'd be waking up to after that night in Vancouver. This is the glimpse of the future I thought I might actually be able to keep. But now, it's just the final moment of a night that was supposed to be about getting the wrong girl out of my system.

Natalie, not Allie.

Natalie Baxter.

Shit, even reminding myself who she is isn't enough to make this suck any less. She might be the absolute worst woman I could pick, but it physically hurts to let her go. So yeah, her plan to work this thing between us out of our system? Total fail.

Not that I really expected anything else. But *damn*, this sucks.

She murmurs my name, reaching across the sheets for me.

Leaning over, I kiss her, soft and slow. Watch as she blinks up at me with sleepy eyes and sifts her fingers into my hair.

"Time to go?" she asks quietly.

"Yeah, baby. Don't want anyone to see me leaving."

She nods but doesn't let me go. I turn my face into her touch, pressing one last, lingering kiss along the smooth skin of her wrist.

And then I back off the bed and force my legs to move until I'm out of her room, out of her place. Gone.

It's for the best.

She might not be out of my system, but we had our night and now I'm going to let her go.

I have to.

Morning skate comes and goes. I give it my all, pay attention when we watch tape, and eat lunch with the team. I work out. But something's off. Hell, when

Baxter bumps into me outside the locker room I don't even think before mumbling a "my bad" and heading out to my car.

He. Bumped. Into. Me.

Baxter.

I'm not saying I should have thrown down, or that any other day I'd even want to. But I'd at least get good and pissed about it. Today, I can't muster the fucks to give.

I can't stop thinking about the look in Allie's big blue eyes before I left this morning, or how she melted into me when she fell asleep the night before. How instead of wanting to chew my arm off to get away, all I wanted was to figure out how I could stay.

Christ, she could absolutely derail my plans without ever meaning to. All it would take is word getting out that I've set my sights on Baxter's little sister and I'd be fucked. The team wouldn't stand for that shit, the fans would villainize me even more than they already have, and Coach would be done. I'd be out.

I'd be throwing away my career, and nothing is worth that. Especially not a girl who doesn't date hockey players. No matter how much I like her.

Natalie

THE THING about coaching a bunch of twelve-year-old girls is while they will laugh until they cry when you do something stupid like tripping over your own skates, once you get up, they flock around you for the group hug of the century. Which is what I'm getting now, and it's almost worth the bruised ass I'm going to have.

I need this.

I need to keep my mind off Vaughn Vassar and pay attention to what I'm doing, because *ouch!* Rubbing my glute while the girls peel off to help pick up the pucks from our practice, I skate over to the bench where George is waiting for me, a wide grin stretching her mouth as she pinwheels her arms in slow motion, bugging her eyes in feigned terror.

"Laugh it up," I say, planting my hands on the boards in front of her. She's doubled over, red hair standing up like flames around her freckled face as she gives in to hysterical laughter.

George isn't a regular coach for my team but comes in to do some one-on-one with our goalie when she can swing it. I was thinking how lucky I was that she could make it tonight, but watching as she swings her arms around again, wheezing out what I'm guessing is supposed to be me shrieking as I went down... hmm.

Finally coming up for air, she wipes an honest-to-God tear from her eye and sighs. "That was classic, Nat. I haven't seen a flail and bail of that caliber from someone over eight in like... *ever.*"

I sigh, waiting for the rest of it. Because, there's

totally more. If she'd been the one to wipe out, I'd have sprayed her with ice and razzed her for the next two hours. "Mmhmm. Just get it all out."

Cocking her head, she sticks out her bottom lip. "I'm sorry. I shouldn't be teasing you after a sprawling, starfish wipeout like that."

Yep, it was a good one.

"Bet your ego has a booboo, huh?"

It's smarting right about now. Correct.

"I mean, *splat*."

Deep breath.

"Think you'll be able to make it off the ice without another wreck?" Making a show of craning her neck, she scans the rink. "I see one of the tot's skating trainers over there." Flashing me an impish wink, she adds, "Just wait here and I'll bring it to you."

"That all you got?" I ask, laughing right along with her.

After a day spent trying to convince myself that what happened with Vaughn last night was enough for me when I know it wasn't—laughing feels good.

"For now, but give me an hour and a couple beers." She plops down on the bench and digs around in the enormous messenger bag she drags around everywhere. When she finds her phone with the spiderwebbed glass, she adds, "Diego and Pete are already at Belfast, and Ted said he'd try to meet us when he's done with the peewee practice."

The beer and company sound good. I haven't seen

George's oldest brother Pete and his husband in months, and Ted is a fun guy. But *Belfast*?

My belly does a little twisty thing that I'd like to think is more nerves than anticipation, but that skip in my pulse and breathless feeling is all about me knowing that Vaughn likes Belfast.

I've already run into him there once.

No one could blame us if we just happened to end up in the same bar.

What would be the harm?

Dang it, I know the harm. Which is why I'm not going.

No more accidental meetings, and definitely no accidentally-on-purpose ones either.

Only, even as I think it, I find myself scanning the windows between the rink and the main hall. Ugh, and that's totally a pinch of disappointment at seeing the glass free of broody NHL players.

George raises a brow. "What, is it Ted?" She lowers her voice, even though the girls have already gone into the locker room and the Zamboni has started its first loop around the ice. "So he likes you, so what? I already told him to forget it. The hockey fanboy is too strong with him. But he's fine just being friends."

"Wait, what?" I shoot a look toward the hall leading to the other rink. "Ted?"

"Yeah. Ted. Light-brown hair, nice eyes, hangs on your every word. Always offering you a ride home from practice. Asks you to grab a drink every time he sees you. *Ted.*" Shaking her head, she throws the phone into her bag and slings it over her shoulder. "Okay, so it's not Ted. There isn't a game tonight. What's up?"

A part of me wants to tell her. Spill the whole shady story right here. George is one of my closest friends. She's been there through my best days when we were winning championships in college and my worst when the doctors told me I was done playing. I love her. I trust her. *But…* This thing with Vaughn isn't something she understands. And I'm already confused enough about my own feelings without bringing hers into the mix.

"Earth to Natalie?" she sings, waving at me like I might have lost her in the two feet of space between us. "You okay?"

"Sorry! Sorry." I meet her eyes and give her the closest thing to the truth I can scrounge up. "Actually, I didn't get much sleep last night." So true. So, so worth it. "You guys have fun tonight, but I think I'm just going to go home and crash."

For a minute, I think she's going to call me on my lie, but she pulls me into a hug instead. With a last smile, she heads out and I duck into the coaches' locker room to grab my shoes. Then drop my skates at the sharpening hutch. I check the schedule pinned to the wall, to see who has ice when.

Killing time, I realize with another guilty pang.

Waiting to see if Vaughn might turn up. If maybe he found another excuse to be where I was. To see me again. But he hasn't… and that's a good thing.

I know it is, even if I can't stop thinking about him.

Chapter 12

Vaughn

I'm not a prick.

That's the excuse I'm going with as I take the short walk up to Natalie's door, my pulse jacked like the puck's about to drop.

We had sex. Hot. Wet. Blow-your-mind sex.

And I'm not looking for a repeat.

I'm not.

I'd have to be a total fuckwad if I showed up here intent on backing her against another wall and catching her breathy moans with my mouth when it's been less than twenty-four hours since we agreed we were only going to do it the one time.

This is about making sure she's okay after last night. Because despite what our track record would suggest, I don't get the feeling *casual* is her style. So it would be shitty not to check in.

It's not about seeing her again. It's about doing the right thing.

I won't even go inside. Hell, maybe I won't even have the option. Her lights are on, but it's Friday at ten p.m. She's young. Single. Has a life full of family and friends.

She's probably not even home.

I rake my hands through my hair. What was I thinking showing up at her place like this?

I should have called. Texted.

Scratch that. I have no idea how her notifications are set up and wouldn't want to risk my mug popping up on her screen while she's hanging out with her douche brother playing Scrabble. And yeah, *Scrabble,* because that's a hell of a lot easier to swallow than the more likely scenario where she's out at some bar getting hit on by every dude with luck enough to share space with her.

I swallow past the fist stuck in my throat at the idea of all those guys moving on her when she's—

Damn it, she's not mine.

I ought to leave. Turn my ass around and go home. Get some rest for the upcoming games.

Rest I don't need because I've already napped today.

And let's be real, the chances of me catching a single wink when I'm thinking about Natalie out with all those assholes scheming to get into her pants? Next to none. Not good on a night before a game. Not fair to the rest of the team. So maybe I'll wait for her to come home. Make sure she gets in okay and she isn't upset about what happened last night. And then I'll go.

Christ, I don't want her to be upset about last night.

An engine revs in the distance, and I take a last look over my shoulder. A few friends are huddled together at the end of the block and a guy on a bike is talking into his earbud mic as he pedals by, but no one seems interested in the bigger-than-average guy standing on Natalie Baxter's stoop.

Not yet anyway.

I knock and suck a long breath through my nose, telling myself to chill the fuck out. I'm going to see her. Eventually. And until then—

The door swings open and... *I'm so screwed.*

"Vaughn," Allie whispers on a shaky breath, the deep blue of her eyes pulling me in. "What are you doing here?"

Yeah, what *am* I doing here?

Because it sure as hell isn't making sure she's okay after last night.

Not the way I'm cataloging every fucking detail about her. The exaggerated rise and fall of her chest beneath a white tank top, the Wisconsin sleep pants hanging just below those sexy hip bones I want to scrape my teeth over. Her pretty little naked toes and soft bare lips.

I take a step forward, put my hand on the doorframe to stop myself. "I'm a total fuckwad."

A surprised laugh huffs past her lips. "Why's that?"

Jesus, she's pretty. "I can't even remember what bullshit excuse I had for coming over here."

"But it was bullshit?" She doesn't seem too upset that I'm here. In a twisted way it would be easier if she did.

"Didn't feel like it at the time. But yeah."

The corners of her mouth tip up the barest degree as she leans into the open door. That hint of a smile changes her whole face, giving her a sexy, playful edge that has me planting my other arm on the frame and gripping it so hard my knuckles turn white.

"Allie." Her name comes low and rough, and pushing out the next words is like forcing gravel and glass past my throat. "Tell me to get out of here and I'll go."

My gut knots as I wait for her to do it. Say it. Tell me to get off her stoop and leave her alone.

She swallows, looking away. "And if I don't?"

It takes a beat before that quietly posed question processes. One painful pump of the organ in my chest while I brace for an impact worse than two hundred pounds of defense coming at me with everything he's got. But when her words register, the ones I'm not expecting, my head snaps up, and every muscle I've had on lockdown since the second she opened the door busts free.

I bury one hand in the soft curls behind her neck as we come together in a hard, clashing kiss that's all deep, sliding tongues, grasping hands, and shuffling feet as we move inside.

"I tried to stay away," I say against her mouth, my breath ragged and strained.

We can't get close enough.

"I tried to want you to." Her fingers knot in my hair, tugging just right. "But it's no use. I was calling you when you knocked."

I pull back to search her eyes. "Yeah?"

"Sorry." She really looks it too.

"Not sorry," I growl. And then we're kissing again, harder, hotter.

I push her tank up and thumb the tight bead of her nipple with one hand while sliding the other over her perfect ass to pull her closer. Her hips tip into the contact and she whimpers.

That sound.

I want it again.

Bending my knees, I get the contact I'm after, my cock rubbing against the thin cotton of her sleep pants. And yeah, it's fucking fantastic.

Her hands grip my shoulders as she meets me stroke for stroke. Moaning and sighing, grabbing my ass, my arms and chest. Pushing to her toes and arching into me. Hooking her leg around my hip and making a whimpering noise that says she can't quite get where she needs to be.

In the next breath, I have her off the floor, pressed against the wall next to the door, her body aligned with mine so when I slide my tongue into her mouth and grind my hips into all that warm softness, she gasps.

I do it again and again, unable to stop to give myself a second to contemplate how far off the rails my plans have gone.

I can't think about anything except how fucking good she feels in my arms. How sweet those little sounds she's making are. How bad I want inside.

"Need to fuck you," I grunt at the feel of her pussy spasming against me.

"I'm on the pill," she gasps, meeting my eyes and searching them with a vulnerability that wrecks me.

"I'm clean." Thank fuck I've been tested, because the idea of getting inside her like this has me ready to blow my load right now. "You sure—?"

But then she's kissing me again, devouring my mouth and moaning when I take back control to devour hers.

I hook my thumbs in the waist of her pants and panties and shove them down her hips as she hikes one leg free while attacking my fly.

And then I've got her by the backs of her thighs, tank top shoved above her gorgeous tits, sleep pants caught around her left knee. I line up, teasing my head through her slick folds as she trembles. "So wet for me."

"Vaughn, I need you."

She has no idea what that does to me. What *she* does to me.

Our eyes meet, holding as I push into her in one deep thrust that has her breath rushing past her lips.

"Okay?" I ask, holding where I am because she's still so tight, I want to give her a chance to adjust.

She nods, lips parted, cheeks flushed.

"Baby, you feel so fucking good."

I can feel *everything*. Each flutter and clingy grasp of her body around me. All that slick, snug heat. *I can feel her heartbeat.* Or maybe it's mine. The only thing I can't feel is where I end and she begins.

"So good," she echoes against my lips, that desperate touch turned soft as she feathers her fingers over my jaw and down my neck. Like all we needed was this.

I start a slow rhythm, sinking as deep as her body will let me go, thrusting against that spot. Every time I bottom out, her pussy clenches around me. Every time I drag myself back, she clings to me with greedy pulls. And every time she looks into my eyes, I'm gone for her that much more. I don't know how we're going to stop this when having her heart beating against mine feels so right.

I can't think about it. Not now. Not when I'm buried inside her and her breath is washing over my neck in soft puffs and her fingers are threaded through the mess of my hair.

Pulling out almost to the tip, I shift my angle and

slide back in.

"Vaughn!"

That's the spot. My name fills the air with a mix of breathy pleas and silent gasps as I work us both toward the edge.

She's almost there. "Need you to come for me, baby."

Using the wall for leverage, I hold her with one hand and slip the other between us to rub my thumb over her clit.

And that's it. Her soft cries fill the space around us as she clamps down on me so good and so hard. I'm barely a stroke behind and then I'm coming inside her, filling her with the part of me I've never shared with another woman.

Pressing my forehead to hers, I breathe her in.

"Allie," I say, pulling back to meet her eyes. So soft and blue. So trusting, when she shouldn't have trusted me at all. "Baby, I'm sorry, but I'm not letting you go."

Natalie

MY BRAIN and body are still reeling from what Vaughn just did to me, so it takes a second for the words to filter through the haze of sex clouding my mind. But then…

"What?"

He means not this minute. Not tonight. And that's

good, because I don't want him to let me go tonight. He's still inside me and already I want him again. Only the gruff apology in his voice warns this isn't about tonight.

"I know it's not what we talked about." He tucks a bit of hair behind my ear. "I know it's fucking complicated. But I've tried, and I can't stay away from you."

My heart does one of those little flips, because it's what I want to hear. Just not what I *need* to hear. This thing between us is a temptation I can't afford. Neither of us can, but for completely different reasons.

Carefully, he sets me down, keeping one hand at my hip as I find my footing. He untangles my tank top and pulls it down to my waist before helping me with the sleep pants and panties pooled around one ankle. How is this man so tender and careful with me, and so shut off and forbidding with everyone else?

I lean back into the wall with a sigh, but neither of us is ready to break the contact. The quiet intimacy. His jaw is rough with stubble beneath my touch, square and stubborn and beautiful. His fingers are light, tracing the divot at my navel. "Vaughn, think about what you're saying."

Turning his jaw into my palm, he drops a kiss there.

"I know this isn't something we can keep. There are too many reasons we can't go the distance. You want a life that isn't dictated by the NHL, and I can't afford to fuck things up here if I want a contract with Oregon next season."

"I wouldn't want you to." I know what hockey means to him. What it means to anyone who's made it to this level in their career. But I need to be as smart as he is, and remember that a life of being prioritized second to hockey is a life I can't let myself live. Not even with a man who affects me the way he does. "I don't want to talk about this. Can't we take tonight and—"

"That's what I'm saying." His hand covers mine and pulls it to rest against his chest. Such a nice spot. "What if we take this time we have. Tonight… and all the nights until the season ends?"

My breath catches and I slowly shake my head. The risk to his career is too much. "What do you think is going to happen when the guys find out about us? Things are just starting to turn around for you with the rest of the team."

"Honestly, I'm starting to think our chances of keeping this quiet might be better if we give in. I'm losing my shit every time I see you and think I can't have you. Every time one of my teammates pulls you into a hug, pretending they don't want anything more than to be friends—which is bullshit, by the way. And the way you're looking at me. Baby, I fucking love it, but if anyone catches that look, we're done."

It's so sweet the way he thinks anyone would be looking at me closely enough to catch whatever look I'm giving him. "I'm not sure how any of that changes if we're together. My friends—*just friends* and that's not bullshit, by the way—are still going to hug me. And the way I'm looking at you? Well, no one is going to notice some look on my face, so maybe that's not really an issue."

He brushes a thumb along the back of my hand. "*I* notice. And then we have to worry about them seeing the look on *my* face too. Allie, telling myself I can't have you when you're right here is killing me. And after what we just did, I'm thinking you don't love it either. So why fight it? Why don't we enjoy what we have while we have it?"

How can he even ask that? "Because your career is at stake."

He gives me that hint of a smile. "And I'll protect my career. I will. No one has to find out about us."

My pulse picks up. There's something anxious and excited pushing at the walls I hide behind. There's a whisper of hope winding its way through me.

I could have this. I could have him. For a few months and then he'll be moving across the country and I'll move on with my life the way I've always planned to. For me it's a low-risk opportunity that gives me a taste of the one thing I've sworn I won't take. The one man I've always wanted.

But for Vaughn… the risk is greater. "I don't know."

"No?" he says, that deep, buried smile emerging even more as he cocks his head at me, eyes gleaming with a new light. Oh God, that look. "Guess I should probably start convincing you then." And he sinks to his knees.

Chapter 13

Vaughn

I am one compelling motherfucker when I put my mind to it. And yeah, I may have put my mouth and hell, the rest of my body, to it a few times too. But truth? Pretty sure Natalie was convinced before I made her come on my tongue the second time and definitely before I had her panting my name in the shower. And by the time I dragged myself out of her place this morning, it wasn't with that brutal sense of finality from yesterday.

It was with a sleepy smile and soft kiss. I'm still thinking about how nice it was on the plane before we take off for Pittsburgh when O'Brian drops into the seat beside me and ruins it.

"What the fuck, man?" I cough, cutting him a sharp look, expecting to see shrapnel from a can of Axe body spray littering his suit. Make that his wrinkled suit. And damn, how many times did this guy cut himself shaving today? He's a train wreck.

"Sorry," he groans as Popov and Diesel swear from the next row back and get up to move. "Bunny incident."

The hell?

"Jesus, another?" Rux asks, walking past with one hand covering his nose. "Why the fuck can't you get a girlfriend?"

"Yeah, like you?" O'Brian fires back, running a hand through his hair. "When was the last time you had a regular girl?"

Rux stops, meets my eyes, all *Can you believe this guy?* before leveling him with a look. "Dude, I'm not the one who smells like I've been dipped in a vat of Dark Temptation."

Rux keeps walking and O'Brian digs his AirPods out of his backpack.

I don't want to know.

Except, I guess I do.

Arms crossed, I jut my chin at him. "What kind of incident we talking about?"

"The kind I shoulda known better than to let happen," he says with a disgusted sigh. He shoves the sleeves up his wrists, exposing two rings of fresh bruises that have me fighting a grin my teammate probably wouldn't appreciate.

"You like being tied up?" Kind of surprising and not my bag, but no judgment.

"No, asshole," he grumbles. "I was trying to be a fucking gentleman."

Wiping my hand over my mouth, I push down the smirk threatening to bust free. "A gentleman?"

"Yeah, man. I'm not a selfish lay. Carmen was into it and I figured why not let her do whatever got her off."

"Uh-huh. So you let her tie you to the bed."

He mumbles something under his breath and my brows shoot to the air vents above us.

"Come again?" This is too good.

"Handcuffs."

"Mmm… And?"

"*And she lost the fucking key*. Or so she said."

Allie is going to love this. "You don't believe her?"

"Well she sure found it pretty quick when it looked like I was going to miss the plane."

Yeah, because there's a cardinal rule amongst the bunnies. Fuck the players, but don't fuck with their game.

The pre-takeoff announcement sounds through the cabin and when it's done I look back to O'Brian who's wearing the kind of pissy look on his face I'm generally known for. I should cut him a break, but I guess I'm feeling sort of affectionate toward him today.

"So this business with the body spray… was that part of the kinky shit she got up to while you were all vulnerable and at her mercy?"

125

Barking out a laugh, he relaxes into his seat. "No, man. I was so late, I couldn't go home. And even coated in a night of dirty sex sweat, no fucking way was I about to give her the opportunity to lock me in her bathroom while I showered. I had this suit in my trunk to get dry cleaned and I ran into a CVS for the body spray and a disposable razor."

"Jesus, you do need a girlfriend."

We start down the runway. "Aww, you applying for the position?"

"Hard pass. And nice try there selling me on your generous lover bullshit, but I've got my pride, man. No way am I competing with all your bunnies." Besides, I've got a girl.

"Yeah." Rubbing his eyes with the heels of his hands, he yawns. "Not the first time I've heard that."

I snort. "Glad you made it. We're going to kick some ass tonight."

Giving me another fist bump, he grins. "Fuck yeah, we are."

I'm ready to knock off for a nap, when something occurs to me. "O'Brian?"

He turns his head against the rest to face me. "Hmm?"

"You had time to wash your hands though, right?"

When he flips me off, I'm pretty sure it means yes. But I make a mental note to get some sanitizer anyway… and take a bath in it.

Chapter 14

Natalie

*T*he first week after we stopped fighting and gave in to this thing between us, I was constantly waiting for the other shoe to drop. Waiting to find someone from the press camped outside my door when Vaughn opened it to leave at four thirty in the morning. Or for him to come to his senses and tell me he had to put hockey first—that I was a risk he couldn't keep taking. But instead, he kept showing up. Devouring my mouth like a starved man, whispering dirty promises against my lips… delivering on them so thoroughly and completely, that by the time he was done, I didn't have the strength to worry about anything at all.

The second week, I realized he was right. No one was watching us.

The press cared about his hat trick in the game against the Maple Leafs and whether tensions were easing between him and Greg. No one caught on to how often our eyes met across the bar. They didn't notice how my cheeks kept turning red from the texts he sent. They didn't see the way he brushed past me in the crowd, close enough that I could feel his cock rub against my ass in a tease so effective it's a miracle I didn't jump him right then.

The third week, I wasn't thinking about anything beyond how many hours it would be before I had his hands on me again. Before he was inside me, making me feel like no one and nothing had ever made me feel. I told Helene, who was ecstatic, and George, who was not. I was laughing out of nowhere, thinking about the way he held me in his lap and told me the latest "Bunny Incident" with Quinn O'Brian and sighing over the stories he'd shared from when he was growing up.

Now we're doing the backward dance we've perfected around road trips, overbooked schedules, and family commitments. My toes barely touching the ground as Vaughn guides me toward my bedroom, pulling me in and up, his mouth barely breaking from mine long enough for air.

We're halfway to my room when I remember the conversation that started before I left for the clinic and bounced from phone to text to video and back again throughout the day. I dig my heels in and press my hands into his chest to stop him.

Having come straight from practice, he's freshly showered, wearing cuffed jeans that hug and hang over the hard-packed contours of his ass and thighs just right, and a navy button-down that's fitted so perfectly it looks like they sewed him into it on the way over. And it takes everything I have not to feel him up over his clothes.

"You don't think it's weird that we've been fooling around this long and I haven't seen your place yet?"

"It's not weird." Flattening his hands over mine, he drags them past his pecs to his shoulders. "Your place is awesome and mine—mine isn't."

God, this guy's body does crazy things to me.

And Vaughn knows it too, because that cocky smirk is in place as he dips down to catch my mouth in another dizzying kiss. His tongue slides past my lips, stroking in and out in a dirty promise that has every part of me tightening in needy anticipation.

Sifting my fingers into the still-damp waves of his hair, I'm about to climb him right here, but I force myself to take a breath instead.

"So I can't even see it? Ever?"

This time when he comes in for a kiss, I pull away.

His brow arches in surprise—and seriously, big, bad, tough Vaughn Vassar's surprised face is kind of adorable. Which makes holding out on that kiss I want so bad even harder. But this thing with his place has gone on long enough. I get it that we can't go out—I don't want to—but my place is so small. And he already said it wasn't a security thing. Apparently his digs are very private.

So it's starting to feel kind of weird that he doesn't want to show them to me.

I cross my arms and shrug.

"Natalie," he growls, giving me the crabby scowl that intimidates everyone who gets within fifty feet of him, but not me. Honestly, it makes me kind of hot, but I still don't budge. And when his head drops forward in defeat, I leap up and shower his neck and jaw with kisses as he bands one arm around me and walks us to my room. "Pack a bag."

———

"IT'S NOT *UGLY*," I say, shrugging off my black puffer coat in the back entry to Vaughn's place. "I mean, it isn't really what I'd have expected for a twenty-nine-year-old professional hockey player with the kind of disposable income you have, but—"

"Babe, it's ugly."

Fine, it is. It's really ugly and not in any cool or intentional sort of way. From the outside it looks like any other graystone. Nice. Garage in the alley. Fenced-in little yard and a covered breezeway leading up to the back door.

But once you get inside… "I don't get it," I finally say, shaking my head at what looks like an amateur rag-rolled zebra-patterned paint job, the brass accents, and

Old-West-themed runners at the top of the walls. "How did you end up living *here*?"

"I told the agent what I needed security- and privacy-wise. And moved in sight unseen."

"Yeah, but you could have had it updated. Painted." I turn to face him. "Isn't it *supposed* to be painted before you move in?"

"I could have changed it," he mutters, stuffing his hands in the pockets of his jeans. "But…"

And then I get it. "But you didn't want to like it. Because Chicago isn't where you want to be." And he's basically counting down the days until he gets to leave.

"Turns out Chicago's not so bad."

Chicago is pretty spectacular. And in spite of his differences with Greg, he seems to have found a rhythm with the team and O'Brian in particular that has Slayers fans everywhere taking notice. But the way he meets my eyes tells me it isn't *just* the city he's talking about.

God, I'm falling so hard. More every minute we spend together.

I know I should be careful. That I'm treading dangerously close to a line I swore I wouldn't cross, to betraying a promise I made to myself when I was sixteen years old getting yanked out of yet another school so we could follow Greg to Dallas. But being with Vaughn just feels too good.

And really what's the harm in letting myself live out this fantasy while it lasts? It's not like I'm going to throw away the life I've spent years building here. I have a job I love, I'm a coach for an amazing team, and a contributor to the community. I have friends and family and plans and priorities, and all of it *means something* to me.

Vaughn means something too. More than I thought he would. But he's a professional hockey player who's signed on to a life of putting the NHL above all else. It will dictate where he lives, what his schedule looks like, activities he can or can't partake in. It will be the thing he has to put first every single time and, to a degree, so will the person who chooses to be with him.

I can't sign on to a lifetime of being second best. It's how I grew up. Second best to my brother. An afterthought to my parents. Barely a consideration in the choices that shaped the lives of our family.

I need to come first. At least part of the time.

I owe it to myself to make good on that promise. Which is why, when the season is over, no matter how much it hurts, I'm going to let Vaughn go.

But until then, I'm going to revel in every dirty kiss, soulful embrace and hard-won laugh this man can give me.

I look up into his gray eyes and pat his chest. "Chicago might not be so bad, but this place *really* is. I can't believe you *forced* me to come over here. A good boyfriend would have protected me."

His head tips back and he laughs, the sound warming me through. After a breath, he asks, "Ready for a tour, baby?"

I push my eyes wide. "You mean there's more?"

"Yeah, but don't get your hopes up."

Dark trim and dated fixtures run throughout the space, but thankfully the wallpaper runners and offbeat paint jobs are limited to the back. Within, beige and browns stretch as far as the eye can see. "Umm… Where's your furniture?"

There's a beast of an L-shaped sectional in his living room, black of course, like the oversized glass coffee table in front of it. But no carpet. No accent pieces. Just an enormous TV mounted on the otherwise empty walls and a pile of gaming equipment stretched across the floor.

It's like he was so pissed that he had to come here, he refused to make the space his own in any way. Like every time he walked in the door, he wanted the glaring reminder that he wasn't staying.

His dining room is more of the same. A massive table that implies at some point in the past he considered having company over. But there aren't any chairs, and the only thing on the table are stacks of paperwork and a few boxes with team memorabilia probably waiting for his autograph.

The kitchen is black and cream. New appliances next to aging cabinets that are mostly empty. The master bedroom… well, there's a bed and another TV. A workout room with all the usual equipment.

And then there's *the room*. The one he almost threw his body in front of when I tried to look into it. The one

I walked into anyway and had to back out of before my head exploded.

"What the heck, Vaughn?" I gasp, peeking in again.

Well, I guess that's where all his furniture went.

Clearing his throat, he rakes his hands through his hair and fists them at the back of his head. "I know. But it felt pointless to find places for everything when I'd only be here for a few months."

At my arched brow, he grunts out, "Fine, more than a few."

Like closer to ten. "You're pretty serious about not getting attached, huh?"

"Not so much as I was." Such a sweet guy.

Inside the room, the scent of cardboard hits me hard. Row after row of neatly stacked, meticulously labeled boxes housing the life Vaughn put on hold until he leaves Chicago fill half the room, while a Tetris-style jumble of furniture fills the other.

I read the labels from the stack closest to where I'm standing: *Trophies—box 3*; *Pucks*; and *Photos.* That's the box I'm itching to get into.

"Can I look?"

Vaughn nods, pushing off the doorframe to stand beside me as I carefully withdraw the top photo and unwrap the packing paper. It's Vaughn and Jesse Garcia helmet to helmet, sweat dripping from their wide, grinning faces.

I brush my thumb over his face and feel my heart taking another little leap in his direction.

"Playoffs two years ago," Vaughn offers, smiling down beside me. "We were on fire that night."

I remember. "You guys have such incredible chemistry. Is it hard playing for different teams after being paired up for so long?"

"Fucking weird. Took me a while to get used to looking back on the ice and not finding him where I expected him to be. And then not having him to shoot the shit with after a game. Yeah, it was hard."

I get the feeling it still is. He's syncing up with Quinn, but it isn't the same. Though I can't help but wonder... if they had the time, if it could be.

"What do you think it is with Garcia that's so different? I mean, I know when I played, there were a couple of girls over the years where it just clicked in a way it didn't with others. But for you?"

Vaughn picks up the box and nods me back out of the room. I think maybe he isn't going to answer but when he sets the load down on the coffee table in the living room, he sits back with a sigh. Shoots me a sidelong look that's almost silly. "I know this is going to be hard to believe, but I don't make friends that easy."

I huff out a little laugh and roll my eyes. "You? Shocking."

"Well it's true. And it's not just with the Slayers." Stretching his arm along the back of the couch, he toys with a curl at my shoulder. "I guess, even when I was little, there was something about how I skated that set me apart. Gave my old man ideas about the kind of player he wanted me to be."

"You don't talk about your dad." I know he passed away a few years ago, but in the time we've spent together, he's never come up. Not even when we talked about my parents.

"Not a lot of good memories there. The guy was an asshole. Didn't want to raise a soft kid, so he set the bar for being hard. Lots of consequences if I didn't perform."

Consequences. My stomach turns, but Vaughn just keeps playing with my hair, winding it around his finger and then letting it go.

"He wanted me to be the best. Made sure I had a reason to see the other kids on the team as competition and not buddies. I never rode with the other kids to the games. Caught hell if he busted me screwing off with them before we played. Couldn't go over to their houses after the games. Pretty soon they weren't asking."

"That must have been hard." I can barely say the word. *Hard* wouldn't begin to cover it. He would have been a year-round player. Hockey would have been his whole life. I was that kind of player. But while my teammates became the only family I could count on, taking care of me and being there for me when my own parents weren't, Vaughn's teammates were the competition.

"It's just how it was." He laughs a little and gives that curl a light tug. "It's why your brother was such a fucking problem for me. I couldn't beat him. And damn, that pissed my old man off. Year after year."

"I'm sorry, Vaughn."

"Don't be. I was as much of an asshole as he was. I could have been different. Stood up to him. But I didn't. Not through high school. Not through college. But then I got called up." He looks into the distance and I wonder what part of that he's seeing. "I was still acting like a dick, looking at everyone like they were trying to take this thing I'd worked for my whole life away from me. One day Garcia skates up to me, throws his arm around my shoulders like I hadn't been the world's biggest prick. He leans in and says, 'Look around, man. You made it. So let's *play*.' I guess it clicked. He was the first guy I played with that I didn't see as a threat. And the relief in that—hell, it was a big deal for me. If I'm being honest, the guy probably saved my sanity along with my hockey career."

My throat is tight, and I can feel the burn of tears threatening behind my eyes. "He's your friend."

He nods and, leaning forward, starts pulling out more pictures. "One of the few."

Chapter 15

Vaughn

We slam into the boards, fighting for the puck in a clash of sticks, pads, and sheer fucking will. The fans are losing their minds because this isn't the first time Mikovanic and I have mixed it up tonight, and with every scuffle, it gets more intense. We both want it. Bad. But I get possession and fire off a pass to O'Brian, shoving clear.

Mik is on me fast, but I'm faster. My quads burn as I give everything I have and a second later I'm there, intercepting O'Brian's return with a one-timer aimed at the six-inch gap making up the path to the net. Their goalie is good, but he's not fast enough and we score.

Satisfaction burns through my veins. My fist pumps and everything fades except the rush and the one face in the crowd I care about.

Allie.

She's on her feet, jumping up and down like a lunatic. For me. I crack a grin she won't be able to see past my mouthguard, but it's there and it's for her. O'Brian and Popov collide with me, clapping my helmet and back and then falling into line as I pass the bench, knocking gloves with everyone.

Her smile is wide. And it feels like the only thing that matters.

It feels like fucking everything.

Five minutes later we've got another win. We're that much closer to making the playoffs.

The guys are jacked in the locker room because this was the best kind of win. One we had to work like hell for. It could have gone either way at any point in the game. But at every turn, we pulled it out.

I get to my phone and see texts from Travis telling me he got wood watching that last play and he'd bet his left nut all the guys over in Oregon did too. He wants to meet with me this week. There's more but I'll read it later. Now I'm scrolling through the texts my girl sent during the game, laughing at her blow-by-blow accounts of action I was a part of on the ice and then checking over my shoulder and shielding the screen when I get toward the end.

Allie: That shot was insane—there couldn't have been more than an inch give on either side!

Allie: I am so hot for you right now. The

dirty things running through my head would make you blush.

Holy shit, I want to know what she's thinking. I want details. But all I've got is my own imagination running off the rails with dirty images of all the things I'm going to do to her.

Allie: There is no way I'm going to be able to make it through an hour at the bar without ripping your clothes off and jumping you in front of everyone. Go, have fun. Then meet me after.

Fuck the bar. The only reason I show up is to see her.

Me: That shot earned me clothes-ripping points, huh?

Allie: We're talking a buttons-everywhere, shirt-in-tatters level event. Maybe switch out the suit for something you don't care about before you come over.

Jesus, I need to adjust my jock.

Me: This suit needs to be replaced anyway. The only thing I care about is celebrating with you.

Two meaty paws land on my shoulders and then I've got O'Brian hanging off my back like a fucking monkey. A two hundred-plus-pound monkey with lightning-fast reflexes and two assists from tonight's game.

"We're gonna be beating the babes off tonight, man. Every piece at the Five Hole is going to be lining up with knee pads and ChapStick just begging for the chance to get on our junk."

I can feel my junk doing a retreat at the thought. There's only one ChapStick girl I'm interested in, and it's got nothing to do with her getting on her knees. Though damn, now that I'm thinking about it—*don't think about it*. Not here. Not with her fucking brother less than ten feet away.

"Sorry, man," I say, shaking him off my back. "I gotta bail."

Head rocked back, he blows out a long breath. "Dude, you don't get it. What happened tonight was magic." He leans in closer, wrapping his arms around me from behind, and croons, "Tell me you felt it too."

I laugh, shrugging him off again to pull on my shirt. "Yeah, I felt it."

It wasn't like it used to be with Garcia. Not really. Though, if I'm being honest, it was pretty close. Different, but not really less.

It felt fucking good.

"That's what I'm talking about. *We're a team.* Together we are greater than the sum of our parts, man. That goes for on the ice and off. Hell, after that play tonight, the girls would do anything if we were together. *Anything.*"

I turn around, lining up my tie, and hell, the hope and desperation in this guy's eyes is priceless. "Has it occurred to you that maybe this kind of talk is why you can't get a normal girl to date you?"

"Oh, yeah. But still. Think about it. *Anything.*"

And now I'm really laughing. "Quinn, I don't want to think about whatever fucked-up kinky shit you think you can't get a bunny to do for you on any given Tuesday. Especially if it's exclusive to me being a part of the deal."

He blinks at me and for a second, I think he might be about to pull me in for a kiss or something, because I don't even know what that gleam in his eyes is.

"You called me *Quinn*," he says like some chick hearing the L-word for the first time. I almost feel bad for backing out on the bar tonight, not because I'd be interested in anything with anyone but my girl. But because this feels good.

From across the locker room Baxter covers one ear, holding his phone up to the other. "Nat! What do you mean you aren't coming? Rux promised to shower and everything."

I turn back to suit up, buttoning my jacket as I fight the grin pushing at my lips. Ruxton Meyers and a couple other guys are making a bunch of disappointed noises before Greg shushes them. "Damn, you need a ride?... Uh-huh, yeah, thanks, Goon... Okay, feel better."

I grab my gear and sling it over my shoulder. I turn to wish O'Brian good luck tonight, but instead of the goofy dumbass crawling all over me from a minute ago, I find all humor gone as the guy's eyes shift from Baxter back to me.

Fuck.

Yeah, and that's guilt chewing up my stomach as the guy walks back to his stall without another word. It sticks with me through my slot with the press and Baxter slapping me on the shoulder with a *"Good game tonight"* he looks like he actually means. It stays with me all the way to my car when I get the next text.

Allie: Want you inside me. Going crazy thinking about it.

And like that it's gone and the only thing I'm thinking is how bad I need her.

Natalie

I DON'T KNOW what's different tonight, but by the time Vaughn texts that he's here, I'm practically shaking. I want his arms around me. His mouth on my neck. His heart pounding against mine.

I want to hear the gruff way he says my name when he knows I'm about to come and I want—*I want him.*

Standing by the couch so my bare legs can't be seen from the street, I wait as Vaughn lets himself in. He looks me over from head to toe and back again and lets out a low growl that sends a deep throb through my center.

"Baby, you didn't." He takes a step forward, stops,

and wipes his hand over his mouth as raw hunger burns in his eyes. "*Christ, you did.*"

"You like?" I ask a little breathlessly, turning around and peering over my shoulder at him.

That growl of appreciation I enjoyed so much when he walked through the door has nothing on the possessive sound he makes when he reads his name across the back of the Slayers jersey I'm wearing for him. "I wish I could have worn this to the game, but if it makes you feel any better... I did wear these." With one arm braced on the back of the couch, I bend forward in a tease, inching the hem of my jersey high enough to show off the results from my deep dive into Etsy.

His eyes zero in on the white cotton panties with his number across the ass.

That whole buttons-everywhere thing happens before I can even blink. Only it's Vaughn tearing his shirt open in the span of the two steps it takes to catch me up against him by banding his powerful arms across my belly. I squeak as he buries his face in the crook of my neck and groans against my skin. "Baby, I like it so fucking much."

Sliding one hand down my leg, he grips the back of my thigh and brings my knee out to the side to rest on the back of the couch. He sinks to his knees behind me and rubs his cheek across the embroidered numbers as his big palms coast over the backs of my legs. "*I love it.*"

Then it's his hands on my ass, gripping and kneading, and his mouth on my thigh, his tongue running wet, slick circles against my bare skin that have me shuddering and pressing back into each kiss. Aching for more, for higher, for deeper.

"Vaughn, I need you," I whimper when he licks a teasing trail up to the edge of my panties and presses a gentle bite over the skin there. My inner muscles clench and then clench again when his mouth moves between my legs where I'm soaked for him.

"So sweet, Allie." Hooking a finger inside, he pulls the panel out of the way and licks into me. "Can't get enough of you." He spears me with his tongue, slow and firm, his fingers digging into my hips. And when I clamp down around him, he moans against my most sensitive spot.

It's more than I can take. Not enough of what I need.

With a desperate cry, I turn and pull him to stand. And then he's kissing the life out of me, feeding me the taste of myself as I thread my fingers into the thick silk of his hair. We're out of control, hands everywhere, tongues clashing, bodies grinding in search of more contact. Hearts pounding hard together.

"*This*," I gasp against his mouth, emotion I can't explain surging through me. "This is what I need."

Pulling back, he meets my eyes, looks down at my mouth and shakes his head. "*You're* what I need."

I swallow past the knot in my throat. Because *yes*.

Our eyes hold a second longer and then we come together in a crush of lips, teeth, and tongues. It's like whatever happened in the course of that one look ratcheted the urgency between us to critical levels.

He's got my knee at his hip, and we're grinding against each other like teenagers. I rock my hips so we line up just right and— "Oh my God! Like that, like that... please."

Giving me another dark growl and the thrust of his steely cock against my clit, he has me teetering on the brink.

And then falling over with a yelp, because I've literally tipped over the back of the couch onto the cushions. Vaughn doesn't miss a beat, following me over so he lands between my legs and grinds against that perfect spot.

With one arm planted beside my head, he grips the arm of the couch with the other, giving himself exactly the leverage to make my head spin.

"More," I gasp, biting at his lips and then moaning around the deep thrust of his tongue into my mouth. So good. "*Harder.*"

"Fuck, baby, you're killing me," he grits out, but he gives me exactly what I'm begging for. Rocking into me hard enough that the couch starts to move, bumping into the end table behind it. A framed picture topples and the remote clatters to the floor.

We laugh into each other's mouths, and everything slows down. Like maybe neither one of us wants to rush past what feels to me like a truly perfect moment.

Sliding my fingers into the dark waves falling

around both our faces, I whisper, "Okay, so maybe *this* is what I need."

There's another thud behind me and Vaughn's head comes up, a question in his eyes. But I don't have the brain power to figure out what else fell or how.

Except that sound wasn't really behind me so much as over by the—

"*You're a fucking dead man!*" Greg's voice booms from the general proximity of the front door.

Chapter 16

Natalie

*G*reg is going to kill him.

Vaughn closes his eyes, his muttered "fuck" barely audible beneath my brother's storming threats. He's backing off me, but not fast enough.

From the slice of space between the side of the couch and the big body still on top of me, I catch the flash of my brother's fist as it connects with Vaughn's cheekbone.

"No!" I scream, struggling to get up, but Vaughn barely flinches, taking the hit in stride.

His big hand centers on my chest, gently holding me in place. "Don't worry," he says. "We'll work this out. Stay here."

Another fist flies, but Vaughn shifts back, shooting

Greg a lethal glare. "Give me a second to get up so we don't hurt—"

"So you can get off my sister, you motherfucker?" The sound that comes out of my brother's throat is like something I've never heard before, and it terrifies me. "*Get off my goddammed little sister!*"

"Greg, stop!"

Again, I try to get up, but Vaughn shoots me a warning look as he stands, facing off with my brother. "Stay on the couch, everything's going to be fine."

Greg laughs, sounding more like a lunatic than the loveable laid-back guy he is 95% of the time. "The fuck it is. First, I'm gonna beat the living hell out of you. And then I'm gonna get on the phone with Coach and your ass is gone. Attacking my sister? There's no fucking coming back from this one. No team in the league will touch you. You're done."

I gasp. "He didn't attack me, you idiot!"

He points a finger at me. "Nat, so help me, not now."

"It's not what it looks like, Baxter. Just take a breath and let me explain."

Greg's jaw clenches hard enough I can hear his molars pop. "Not one word." He grabs the open sides of Vaughn's torn shirt. "You don't say one fucking word about her, about this."

I scramble from my seat and two sets of angry eyes cut to me as both men speak in unison. "Stay back."

I take a staggering step toward the corner with the TV.

Vaughn's fists are balled at his sides, but even after Greg threw the first punch, this man who lives to fight with my brother hasn't laid a hand on him. Yet. It's because of me, but everyone has a limit. And Greg has nothing holding him back and a righteous sense of indignation pushing him forward. It's a powder keg of testosterone in here and the air practically crackles with aggression. I know the kind of damage these two could do to each other, and inadvertently, anyone caught in the blast radius.

"Okay, I'm back. But Greg, let him go and let me explain."

Greg doesn't even look at me when he answers. "Probably safer for this fucker if you don't."

Vaughn scoffs, blowing out a disgusted breath. "Baxter, this isn't about you. In fact, it's none of your goddammed business. So why don't you get your hands off me and back the fuck up."

"Make me." The pure menace in his voice makes me sick. These men are too close of a match. They're too tough to go down easy, too big to think the damage won't be significant, and too stubborn to just let it go.

"Should I?" The smirk on Vaughn's face is nothing like the one he gives to me… it's backed up by fifteen years' worth of bottled aggression just waiting for release. And right now, he's got the perfect opportunity to let it loose.

Greg gets within an inch of his face and roars, "My fucking sister!"

Regret replaces the brewing violence in Vaughn's eyes, and when Greg's fist comes back again, he doesn't even move. A scream breaks free of my lungs as another brutal punch lands on Vaughn's face. But again, all he does is give a small shake of his head.

Greg's nostrils flare with every breath, the look in his eyes wild. "There are rules, asshole! There are lines you don't cross. I know you don't like me and the feeling is mutual, but we're on the same fucking team and you do *this*?"

Vaughn's had enough. He shoves Greg off. "I know she's your sister. And that's why I let you have not one, but two free throws. Now get your shit together and listen, because you won't get another. This isn't about you. I tried to stay away from her… but I couldn't."

"Is that supposed to be a fucking excuse? You tried? Fuck you," Greg spits. He's pushing for violence, just like he was that day at the start of the season.

My heart stops as guilt rips through me.

I can't let it happen.

Both of them want me far away from the conflict on the brink of exploding, but I push forward. Heart slamming, I rush between them, putting a hand on both their chests.

"Greg, stop. I'm not some victim here, so don't try to paint me like one. I wanted this. For crying out loud, look at my shirt. It's got his name on it! We're together.

This really isn't about you." *Please don't let him see the panties.*

There's pity in Greg's eyes as he looks to me. "I know you think this is real. And I'm so fucking sorry that you got caught in the middle, but believe me, the only reason this asshole is with you is to *fuck with me*. He doesn't care about you, Nat. He's using you."

Vaughn's hand closes over mine at his chest. "He's wrong."

I know he is. But it doesn't make what Greg's saying any easier to hear. Throat tight, I look my brother in the eyes and find my voice. "I know this might be hard for you to understand, but it *is* possible for a guy to want to be with me *because of me*."

"Yeah, Nat, *just not this guy*." Greg grabs my upper arm, trying to pull me out from between the two of them. "You need to go to your room and put some fucking pants on. I'll handle Vassar." I know what he wants, to take me out of the equation, but that's not how it's going to work. I'm a part of this, as much as either of them. And I'm not going anywhere.

I dig my heels in.

His grip tightens and I wince.

The air in the room changes and then it's Vaughn with his hands on Greg, and his face a mere inch away. It's his voice that's laced with deadly intent. "Get your fucking hand off of her before I put my fist through your throat."

Greg's eyes flash to the too-tight hold on my arm.

Instantly he releases it, shaking his head as he apologizes. Not because Vaughn made him, but because that's not the guy Greg is. He would never willfully hurt me or any other female. But I'm still glad he let me go. I'm not his ten-year-old little sister in need of saving, I'm a woman and I have something to say.

I didn't want to have to do this, but Greg needs a reality check. "Vaughn didn't even know who I was the first time I came on to him." I feel Vaughn's chest twitch under my touch, but don't look at him. Technically I wasn't so much the pursuer as the pursuee, but for tonight's purposes that's a clarification we don't need to make. "He had no idea I was your sister."

"So he'd like you to believe," Greg bites back. "I talk about you. Everyone knows I have a sister."

Another grunt from Vaughn. "Believe it or not, Baxter, but I'm not hanging on your every word."

I shoot Vaughn a stern look and grumble, "Not helping." Then turning back to my brother, I take a deep breath. "Yeah, but when I met him almost a year ago, he wasn't on this team. We weren't even in this country, and I told him my name was Allie."

"You what?" Greg blinks, his brows plowing together as his chin pulls back. "Wait, are you telling me this has been going on for a *year*?" He rakes a hand through the short waves of his hair. "You've been screwing this guy behind my back when *I know* you know who he is. I know you remember what a total fucker he was—since he was fifteen fucking years old. Number 26 from East."

Between the disapproval in his look and the betrayal in his voice, I feel lower than low. But this situation needs to be defused as quickly as possible. He needs to know the truth.

"To me he was someone else, okay? He always has been. And when I saw him after that game, yes, I knew who he was, but I didn't want him to know who I was... because I wanted him to like me. But he didn't even know who I was until about a month into the season. And then... well, we became friends."

I'm pretty sure my brother doesn't need me to elaborate on the details. He already looks shell-shocked, so I leave it at that. "Greg, I appreciate you looking out for me. But I think I've made it clear that it's not necessary. I was on a date and I'd like to finish it."

Again, I feel a quake in Vaughn's chest, but I'm pretty sure this one is a laugh he's trying not to let out.

Greg gapes at me. "You want *me* to leave? Leave him... here with you."

I let out a humorless laugh. "Yes. I know sometimes it feels like the whole world revolves around you, but occasionally, it doesn't. This is about me and the guy I've been seeing. A guy who didn't take advantage of me and had the self-control not to break your nose after you sucker-punched him, *jerk*. So I'd appreciate it if you would walk out of here without giving me a hard time. And I'm asking you, *as my brother*, to have enough respect for me, my privacy, and my choices not to share this with the team, and particularly your coach."

Greg looks from me to Vaughn and back again, scrubbing his hand over the back of his head. One heavy breath later, he raises his hands, palms out. "Fine, whatever you want, Nat." Raking a loathsome look over Vaughn, he shakes his head. "When this guy fucks up, I'm just a phone call away."

Taking my brother's arm, I walk him to the door. "Good night, Greg."

***

Vaughn

I'VE NEVER BEEN MORE in awe of someone than I was just now watching my girl face off against her brother. But the second that door is closed, whatever steel was in her spine crumbles and she starts to shake.

Only a step behind, I gather her up in my arms and carry her into the bedroom. This night is done. It didn't go the way we'd planned. And the implications of what happened are—fuck, something I can worry about when I'm done worrying about her.

Climbing into bed, I lean against the wall and hold her on my lap. Her arms are around my neck and I'm rubbing her back with slow strokes, waiting for the racing of her heart to slow.

Finally, she whispers, "I've never seen anyone take a punch like that. You barely even blinked."

Tucking my chin, I look down into her eyes and let out a low chuckle. "Your brother punches like a little girl."

It's not true. The guy wields that fist like Thor's hammer, but I'm fucking hard-headed.

She snickers and relaxes against me. We sit like that for a few minutes, quiet while all the shit from the last hour works its way around my head.

"I'll talk to him tomorrow," she says, unraveling her arms from my neck and smoothing her hands over the remains of my open shirt. "He's not going to take this to your coach."

I don't want to tell her that I think she's wrong. That I'm pretty sure he didn't even make it as far as his car before tattling to the guy with the power to end my career. That I have no idea what this means for my future, and I don't even care because I'm holding her right now, and that's the only fucking thing that matters.

So instead, I tip her head back for a quiet kiss. "Whatever happens, it'll be fine."

Her palm cups my jaw and a sort of unholy light fills her eyes. "Trust me. You don't even want to know the kind of shit I have on Greg. There's no way he's talking to your coach."

I stay until four, holding Natalie against me until it's time to leave. I don't have her confidence about Baxter keeping his mouth shut, but on the outside chance she's right, better to err on the side of caution.

I need to sleep, but I need to do something else first. So after a quick shower and change, I hop back in my car and head a few miles north. O'Brian lives in one of those high-rises down by the lake, and when I text that I'm parked around the corner, he meets me on the street five minutes later.

Dressed in a pair of joggers, hat, and an insulated jacket, he nods toward the lakefront and we start to walk. "Considering I've invited you to my place a dozen times and you've turned me down every one, I'm guessing this is pretty serious. You get traded?"

I shake my head, blowing out a breath that fogs the frigid air. "No. Not yet, anyway. But that thing last night…"

He stops walking and closes his eyes. "Oh shit, tell me you didn't knock her up. Because if you did? It's been nice knowing you. Baxter will hunt your ass to the end of the earth."

"She's not pregnant." Though that spot in the center of my chest that's been acting out since Vancouver feels a little funny at the thought. Not funny bad, which is fucking crazy. But not why I'm standing outside when it's not even a handful of degrees above freezing and the sun's barely broken the horizon. "Baxter knows."

"Fuuuck."

"That about sums it up."

We start to walk again and I tell him what happened, skimming over the details of what he walked in on, and the gist of how it went down after.

He squints at me. "But you didn't knock him back?"

"Come on, man. She's his little sister." Hell, I might actually respect the guy more for wanting to protect her.

"Don't get me wrong. You had it coming. Just wasn't sure you'd see it that way."

There are a few runners out, but otherwise the paths are mostly empty. Even with the skeletal trees and cutting wind, it's pretty. Relaxing to be by the water. It's the kind of place it would have been nice to bring Natalie to if she'd been any other girl than the one she is.

"How'd you leave it? I mean, I'm guessing Greg isn't looking for you to put a ring on his sister's finger. But any declarations made to smooth his feathers?"

Declarations?

He shakes his head in disbelief. "You tell him that you love her? That she's coming to Oregon with you at the end of the season?"

"She's not coming to Oregon." And as to the other? I haven't said it to Natalie yet, so I'm sure as fuck not telling O'Brian or Baxter first. "Don't get me wrong, if I thought it would make her happy, I'd be all about her moving with me. But this is her home."

"Give it time, man. She'll come around."

I'm not up for rehashing all the reasons I know she

won't, so I clear my throat and get to what I came to say.

"Look, Quinn, I know I can be an asshole. I didn't want to be in Chicago and I wasn't much of a team player. But you were relentless and—" I clear my throat, hating what a pussy I sound like right now but knowing it has to be said. Especially because there is a very real possibility we won't be playing together anymore. "Hell, thank you for that, because we played some fucking amazing hockey together. And if I screwed that up, then I'm sorry, man. You deserved better."

Quinn rubs a hand over his mouth and nods, staring out at the lake. Then cutting me a sidelong look, he says, "So I'm thinking this is my window for guilting you into some of the kinky shit I get up to, right?"

I cough out a laugh. "Jesus."

"Admit it, you're dying for details."

Not even close. But man, I'm hoping like hell I haven't blown my chance to finish out the season with this guy.

Chapter 17

Natalie

*V*aughn's been gone for two hours already when I get up. I could have slept the whole day, but I need to see Greg and I want to do it before practice. After a quick shower, I pull on a pair of leggings and a Wisconsin sweatshirt, throw my hair back in a messy knot and head to Dunkin' Donuts. Then, using my keycard and some sweet talk for Joe down in the lobby, I let myself into Greg's place. Standing at his bedroom door, I take a donut hole from the bag and whip it at the lump in his bed.

"Ow!" he grunts as I flip on the lights. Eyes closed, of course. Julia's out of town, but Greg sleeps naked and one of us being scarred for life is enough.

"What the fuck, Nat!" he coughs amid a shuffle of sheets.

"What? I thought we let ourselves in to each other's places these days."

"*I thought you were sick.*"

I pop a donut hole in my mouth and then wing another one in the direction of his voice.

"Fuck! Knock that shit off."

I don't think so. "Put your nuts and berries away. I want a word."

He brushes past me, wearing a pair of Slayers sweats, and grabs the bag out of my hand.

"Hey, those aren't for you to eat."

The scowl he throws over his shoulder satisfies the little sister in me immensely, and I follow him back to the kitchen where I've left the coffees. He sweeps his off the counter and jerks a chair out from the table, dropping into it with a sour grunt.

Standing at the counter, I take a sip of my own. He looks up at me with that pissy, expectant stare, but I did my explaining last night. Besides, everyone knows the one to talk first loses.

My brother might be the hotshot NHL player, with three years and a hundred pounds on me, but I'm not his pushover.

The guy makes it about thirty seconds before slumping back into his chair.

"Fine, fuck it." He throws a hand out to the side. "I shouldn't have barged in there and beat the fuck out of your shady hookup."

I raise a brow and take another sip. "Is that what

happened?" Because I'm pretty sure Vaughn let him pop him twice as a courtesy. And while normal humans might need a trip to the ER after a blow from my brother, Vaughn didn't bat an eye. And when I kissed him goodbye this morning, there wasn't even a bruise.

Greg's jaw tics, and I figure I've got as much of a victory as I'm going to get. Joining him at the table, I grab a donut hole. "You can't go to your coach with this. You and Vaughn don't have to get along, you never have before. But you need to be able to play on the same team, because like it or not, he's really good."

"Don't turn this around on me, Nat. He's the one who fucked our team when he started fucking *my* little sister."

He still can't accept that Vaughn might be with me for any reason other than him. It's an unfortunate side effect of so many years in the spotlight.

Only even as I think it, I realize that not all players are like that.

Vaughn isn't.

Still, I need to work with what I have. "I understand that you're upset. But look at what your team is doing this season. Look at what Quinn and Vaughn did in the game last night."

Scrubbing the back of his head, he blows out a harsh breath.

Translation: *Yes, they really tore it up. Vassar is a true asset to the team.*

"You guys have a solid chance at the Cup. Everyone

is talking about it. But what do you think happens if Vaughn is suddenly up and gone?"

He scowls at the ceiling.

Translation: *I may not like it, but I know you're right.*

"You owe it to the fans, Greg. You owe it to the team. And you owe it to yourself to put your differences aside. Because you're the *captain*."

"Jesus, enough."

Okay, so I might have been overselling that last part a bit.

Arms crossing over his chest, he leans over the table. "Why him? Seriously, Nat, were you pissed at me or something? I mean, yeah, I know it was rough getting yanked out of a school you liked because of me. I know Mom and Dad shortchanged you in a lot of ways. But you know I did everything I could to make that up to you when I had the chance. Are you still mad?"

And dang it, he looks kind of devastated right now and I don't think I can take it. Because even with the way he acted last night, he's not a bad guy. He's one of the best, with a heart so big, sometimes it overwhelms me.

"Greg, this thing with Vaughn has nothing to do with being pissed at you. It never did." Yes, I was angry when we had to move so Greg could be on a competitive team where he'd have a chance at getting noticed. And getting pulled again going into my junior year sucked. I'd been picked as captain and it didn't matter because Greg had been picked to play for the

NHL. It was hard being his sister sometimes, but I didn't resent *him*. "The thing is, when you ask me *why him*… it wasn't about being pissed at you, but I lied when I said it wasn't about you at all. At least for me."

One thick brow arches. "Explain."

"Look, I love you for caring enough about me to look out for me with guys, but even at fourteen that protective streak made dating a little rough."

"Rough how? What the fuck were you going to do at fourteen?"

I pat the air between us, signaling him to chill.

"Rough like, all you had to do was look at a guy and he'd be ready to pee himself. I've got news for you, watching your dates or prospective dates cower at the mere mention of your brother's name isn't hot. And even once you weren't around—"

"What?" His eyes narrow and he leans forward. "Did some asswipe decide to act tough because I wasn't around to do anything about it?"

This from the guy who took it upon himself to meet with the varsity hockey team in my new school and ask them for "a favor." To make sure no one tried to take advantage of me. Those guys had a freshly minted NHL player showing up to talk to them. He knew their names. And he had their loyalty. "No, Greg. In fact, the two or three times a guy was dumb enough to show an interest in me, we suddenly had half the hockey team hanging around watching. And, rest assured, they would have taken a puck to the teeth before asking me out themselves."

He grins. "You're welcome."

"Whatever. It was fine. I didn't date, but it wasn't terrible having half the hockey team adopt me. I'm still friends with most of them today. Stood up in six of their weddings and am godmother to one's daughter."

"How's little Shana doing these days?"

"Still too small to do anything but use that mini hockey stick you gave her to gum on." Thumbing through my phone, I find the most recent picture from last week for him.

He grins but isn't distracted for long. "I get why someone like Vassar might have appealed to you in high school. He didn't intimidate easy and he was outside my circle of influence. But I was out of the picture by college and it's not like I'm warning guys off you these days either. So why him?"

There's no holding back my laugh. "Out of the picture? Greg, you're an international sports celebrity. There is no out of the picture. In college, the guys I dated weren't interested in talking to me about *my* game. They wanted to talk to me about *your* game. They wanted to hear about you. And as for now… You're not warning guys off me, huh?"

He gives me a sheepish shrug but has the sense not to open his mouth.

"Let's forget about Vaughn for a moment. And for the sake of argument, say if Rux, your best friend and

all-around good guy, decided he wanted to date me…
you'd be okay with it?"

The answer is *no*. And knowing Greg, probably
more like *fuck, no*. But being the stubborn type that he is,
my brother won't give. Eyes locked with mine, jaw
clenching and unclenching, he tries to make himself tell
me something other than the truth we both know. In the
end, he shovels four donut holes in his mouth at once.

"Don't worry, bro. I'd never date Rux, and he'd
probably puke down his chest just thinking about dating
me. The surrogate sibling thing is strong with him."

Visibly relieved, Greg washes down his donuts with
his coffee.

"So that's what this boils down to with Vassar? You
like him because he's not afraid to go head-to-head with
me, and you *think* he isn't dating you just to get to me."

"I know he isn't dating me to get to you, because he
could have done it a hundred times already. He could
have thrown me in your face at every turn. Taunted you
with the dirty details from that night in Vancouver—"

Greg's out of his chair so fast it falls over, his fingers
in his ears as he sings, "La la la la…" at top volume.

Oops.

Slapping a hand over his mouth, I meet his
panicked eyes. "Sorry. But my point is this, he didn't do
any of that. And if you really want to know *why him*? It's
because *I like him*, Greg. A lot. I always have."

The donut holes are gone and Greg's coffee is
empty. Clearing them from the table, he dumps them in

the trash and props a hip against the counter. "So, what? Are you guys serious?"

There are so many ways I could answer him. Because the way I feel about Vaughn… yeah, it's serious. More serious than it should be. But— "He's leaving at the end of this season."

"Oregon." Everyone knows the plan.

I smile, because that's what I need to do.

"But even if he wasn't, I'm not interested in making the NHL WAG list. I'm not trying to guilt you or make you feel bad, but I'm through giving up my life because it's not as important as someone else's hockey career. Vaughn knows how I feel. He gets it. So with this thing between us… *serious* isn't an option."

Greg looks like he just smelled rotten milk. "Let me get this straight… you're saying you've got rules about guys like him." He gulps. "You don't date *players*?"

"Normally, no." Whatever that half-panicked, half-stricken look is, I don't get it. "Um, you okay?"

He's big and strong, sure, but the guy is a softy at heart, and I feel kind of crummy about what he's been through in the last twelve hours. Whether my relationships are any of his business or not, this is my brother.

"Yeah, I'm fine. It just sounds familiar is all. Nat, I get why you wouldn't be interested in the kind of life that comes with dating a pro. I know what it was like for you growing up. You didn't have a choice in how things went down then, and it makes sense that you wouldn't want to put yourself in that position again. You deserve to come first."

He joins me at the table, nothing but sincerity and concern in his eyes. "But here's the thing—and believe it or not, what I'm about to say has nothing to do with the guy you're dating being Vaughn Vassar—you are playing with fire."

I sit back. "What do you mean?"

"I mean if you want a life that isn't dictated by hockey, then don't date a hockey player. Not for one week and definitely not for the better part of a year. Don't tell yourself it isn't serious when it's serious enough that you've been lying to everyone you know to keep it secret. When it's serious enough that even with the kind of consequences Vassar has on the line, you still couldn't stay away from each other."

"Consequences that aren't going to be an issue because *you're not going to say anything*." I'd hoped it wouldn't come to this. "Don't test me on this. You know you don't want that Easy-Bake Oven story getting out."

He jerks back like I've slapped him. "Jesus, Nat, I'm trying to help you here! And case in point, serious enough that you're ready to blackmail me with twenty-year-old dirt to protect your boyfriend!"

"It's his career!" I shout back, guilt making me defensive. But I know he's right. Mumbling, I add, "It's that important."

We stare each other down for a minute before Greg lets out a growl and gives me a crabby look. "I already told you I wouldn't say anything. And I won't. But listen, okay? Guys like Vaughn, hell, guys like *me*—we like to win. The girl, the game, the fight. All of it. We thrive on challenges and get off on overcoming odds. And when we find something that matters to us, really matters, we are relentless. And if you don't believe me, ask Julia how *serious* she meant to get about me. Ask her about the rules I broke and the plans she changed— because guess what, she didn't date players either. But ask her how willing I was to let her go and then look at the ring on her finger and ask yourself if you want to risk letting fucking Vassar put one on yours."

"We aren't anywhere close to that," I whisper, a new sort of tension building in the pit of my stomach.

"You sure about that?" Greg looks down at his hand, rubbing his thumb over his wedding band. "Because the way I see it, if Vassar is actually into you for you, every minute you spend with the guy is a threat to the kind of life you've been promising yourself since you were old enough to recognize how bad you needed to break free of mine. Nat, what if you fall in love with this guy? What then?"

I open my mouth to protest, to tell him it'll never happen. That I'm smarter than that. But I can't.

Chapter 18

I don't know what to expect when I get to practice that afternoon. Pulling into the cold gray lot, I sit in the car with the heat blasting for ten minutes, one fucked-up scenario after another running through my mind. Will I even make it into the locker room or will Coach have someone waiting for me on the other side of the doors, ready to pull me into a meeting to tell me I'm done?

The text from Natalie this morning said I didn't need to worry. But it's easier for her to trust Baxter than it is for me. Either way, I need to get my ass into that building and face the future.

Hefting my bag over my shoulder, I walk through the player doors and nearly shit myself seeing Coaches Adkins, Mateo and Channing huddled together at the foot of the stairs. Each wearing an expression darker than the next.

My gut turns to lead, but if this is how it's going down, then so be it. It fucking sucks, but I can't find it in my heart to regret what happened. Maybe that'll come after they walk me out of here. Or when I'm hearing the score from the next game, but I'm not playing.

My eyes are glued to the unhappy trio, so I don't notice Popov until he's beside me, mumbling something about this being very, very bad around some heavy sighs laced with an Eastern European accent.

Shit. He's already heard.

But if so, what's he doing walking with the condemned man?

O'Brian ducks out of the locker room and jogs over. "You hear about Whitney?"

Our third-string forward was fine after last night's game. He's a good kid, kind of quiet. "What happened?"

"Started feeling off after the game, ended up in the ER this morning getting his appendix out."

I look around the lobby, and now I see it. Everyone's noses buried in their phones. Worry etching their brows.

"Oh shit."

"Tell me about it. He ought to be out of surgery pretty soon, but we're all waiting to hear."

Just then Adkins breaks away from the group, disappearing down the hall where the assistant coaches' offices are located. Mateo blows a whistle to get everyone's attention. "Sean Whitney is out of surgery and doing well. More updates as available, but for now everyone get your ass ready for practice."

Popov grins and slaps me on the back while rubbing the top of O'Brian's head. "Good news. He be back on ice in three days."

We nod, because why not? Ericsson did it in '09. And while most players take a little longer than that, why not hope for the best? Which is pretty fucking ironic thinking, considering my attitude walking in here today.

Heading into the locker room, I find Baxter already dressed, dripping sweat after some drills. "Got a minute?"

He gulps down half a bottle of water and tells Rux he'll catch up with him in a few. "What do you want?"

Natalie. And to keep playing through the end of the season.

And if he's asking, I want to be first line and he can be *third*. But mostly I want to make sure this guy isn't going to cause problems over what happened last night. "You need another swing at me or are we good?"

He huffs out a short laugh, looking away before meeting me with a smile that's just a little too cocky for my taste. "We're good. And the only thing I need is for you to kick ass in every game we've got. When your contract comes up, I want Oregon to make an offer that'll get you on a plane that day."

Away from his sister.

Looks like Baxter found the incentive he needed to make it work with me for the rest of the season.

NATALIE HAS evening appointments at the clinic and a late ice time with her team, so it's after ten by the time I pick her up at the rink. I'm not nuts about a six-day road trip after this shit with her brother, but it's not like I can call in sick.

She climbs in the passenger seat and I take her bags and swing them into the back. I want to pull her into me. Kiss the shit out of her and soak up the feel of her against me for a few minutes, but blocking traffic to make out isn't exactly keeping a low profile.

"How's Sean?" she asks, as I merge into traffic.

"O'Brian and I stopped over with some of the other guys to see him this afternoon. He's doing good after the surgery, but you can see the worry." He doesn't have the endorsements yet. The savings. "Doesn't matter that the numbers and the doctors are all on his side, he's freaked out. Getting back on the ice is the only thing that can fix it."

We're quiet through most of the ride, and I can't help but feel like something's off. Like somehow Baxter is sitting between us. I don't want him anywhere near this thing with Natalie and me, so I bring us back to where we ought to be, asking about work and practice.

She tells me about the game coming up for her girls.

There's a longstanding rivalry between the teams and the other coach sounds like a total dick.

"Damn, I'd love to see that game."

Natalie laughs quietly beside me. "Yeah, I bet."

I shoot her a look, but she turns to her window. "I'm fucking serious. I'd love to see your team in action. See how you're shaping these girls' game play. In fact, I'm going to."

"Pretty sure you've got a date with the Predators in Nashville that night."

"You guys record the games?" Now I've got her attention.

"Some," she says hesitantly. "I try to get parents or siblings to sign up, but it doesn't always pan out."

"Don't worry about this one. I'll set it up. Then you'll have some tape to watch with the girls and I'll get to see *my girl* in action." When she stares at me with a look that I think is happy but almost seems sad, I reach across the console and take her hand. "When I want something, I find a way to make it happen. Just wait and see."

Okay, there's definitely something up with that look. Even moving into the more residential area near my neighborhood where there aren't so many lights, I can see it.

"What? You don't believe I'll watch?" I'm going to watch the shit out of her game. Hell, maybe I'll hire someone for all of them.

"No, I believe you."

That's good, right? So why have I suddenly got the fucked-up sense that it's a bad thing?

Natalie

VAUGHN CAN TELL something's off with me. It's in the way he's watching me as I pretend to watch highlights in the living room he wouldn't decorate because he didn't want to get attached to it. It's in the way he holds me when we go to bed—tight, like he wants to hold me forever.

It's in that last questioning look before he kisses me goodbye the next morning. But all I can hear is my brother's warnings still in my head.

God, I don't want to let him go.

I don't want Greg to be right. I don't want him to take anything else I love away from me.

But even as I think it, I know that's not fair. Greg isn't about to take anything from me. All he's doing is asking me to think about what I want and whether what I'm doing is going to get in the way of it.

Sitting on the edge of the step down to my living room, I send the video call I've been avoiding making all day.

I'm about to hang up when Julia's sunny face fills the screen. "Natalie! How's the pregame going?"

She's in LA for a few interviews this week and,

based on the mirror and lights behind her, I think she might be in make-up getting ready to shoot. "Oh no, are you at the studio? This can totally wait," I rush, suddenly wanting to avoid this call.

She waves me off. "Don't worry. I've got time. My player is running late. What's going on?"

Staring at the screen, I tell myself I've already called her. Greg told me to ask, and if something in his warning hadn't resonated just a little too clearly I wouldn't have thought twice about it. But here I am the next day, still hating the way his words made me feel.

Hating that he might be right.

I take a deep breath and start. "This may not be any of my business, so you can totally tell me to buzz off and I won't have my feelings hurt."

Julia pulls a face. "Geez, what do you want to know?" She leans closer to the screen, her eyes going cartoon huge. "Is it something about sex? Oh man, your brother would lose his shit. I mean I won't tell him, but still—" Her head tips back and, eyes closed, she lets out a delighted laugh.

"I kind of hate to disappoint you, but it's nothing like that."

Popping her bottom lip, she shrugs one shoulder. "Okay, let's have it then."

"Greg said something yesterday about you guys and I can't get it out of my head."

"Sounds serious."

And that's the problem. "Jules, you and Greg always

seem happy. Like, deliriously so. And Greg, oh my God. It's actually pretty embarrassing how happy he is. But… he said I should ask you about how things started with you guys. How serious you meant to get about him. And how maybe he broke some of your rules." I can feel the heat pushing into my cheeks, because this feels like none of my business, but now that I've started, I can't hold the words back. "I know you love him. I do. But I guess what I'm asking is if you have any regrets?"

Suddenly all silliness is gone and Julia's waving someone I can't see off as she moves to a more remote corner of the studio. "Nat, honey, where's this coming from? Is this about that guy from out of town?"

Of course she remembers. I smile, but the way hers disappears tells me she can see right through me. "Let's say this is about me, okay?"

Her brown eyes are filled with questions, but she doesn't voice them. "Greg wasn't part of my plan. In fact, my playbook was pretty specific about avoiding guys like him altogether."

"Pretty-boy players with egos so big they need a U-Haul to help drag them around?" I tease, even though nothing feels funny to me right now.

She snorts, shaking her head with a smile. "Actually, it was more geared toward pro athletes. But yeah, even back in high school I had your brother's number. Other girls threw themselves at him left and right, but to me? Guys like him just seemed like a risk I wasn't interested in taking."

"I can imagine." Being a sports reporter—a woman in a predominantly men's field, she faced scrutiny her male peers seldom did. "So what happened? What made you give him a chance?"

Her eyes take on this faraway look and she bites her lip. "It wasn't really *a chance* per se. It was just supposed to be one kiss. But that *kiss*…"

Geez, I can see the goosebumps come up on her arms through my phone. "And that kiss was it? You were gone for him?"

"Not even close. There's a whole story there, but suffice it to say… despite my best efforts to prevent it, your brother worked his way into every part of my heart. And once he was there—" she flashes me one of those eternally satisfied smiles and sighs, "—there was no getting him out."

I nod, not trusting my voice to carry past the lump in my throat. She's happy. No question. But she's also just confirmed my brother's warning. Julia had no intention of letting him into her life and now they're bound together until death do they part.

Chapter 19

Vaughn

"Hey beautiful, sorry I missed you." I yawn into her voicemail, scrubbing a hand over my face as I fight the gravitational pull of my bed after going into overtime against the Knights. "Gotta hit it tonight but give me a call when you get a chance tomorrow."

"GOT YOUR TEXT, babe. Sounds like a crazy day, but glad you're getting some sleep. Call me tomorrow. I want to hear your voice."

"ALLIE." I press my forehead against the cool glass of my hotel room window, closing my eyes to the glittering city lights below. "What's going on?"

She isn't going to answer. It's voicemail again.

She hasn't called me back since I left four days ago and she hasn't texted me in two. Before everything blew up with Baxter, we were talking and texting and finding ways to see each other no matter how jacked our schedules were, so this isn't about being busy.

I take a breath and rub at the aching spot in the middle of my chest.

"You'll laugh at this, babe. I actually had to ask your brother if he'd heard from you. Oh man, it *sucked*. That dude is a stone-cold gloater. Can't remember the last time I've seen him smile that big. He told me he talked to you around lunch and I kept waiting for the pissed to kick in, you know? But Christ, Allie, all I felt was relieved. Yeah, you're dodging me and I don't know why, but you're okay. And that's what matters."

I walk back to the bed and, more beat than I can remember, drop back onto the spread. "So, uhh, look, in case I don't talk to you... Trevon uploaded the footage from your game. Congrats on the win. That play in the second with thirteen and twenty-three was badass. Your girls have the moves. Anyway, it was fun to watch."

ALLIE: **Can we talk?**

Me: About to take off. Be at your place in six hours.

Natalie

I'M WAITING on the stoop when Vaughn comes up the walk still dressed in his suit, a ball cap resting low enough that I can't see his eyes until he's standing in front of me. And then I wish I couldn't because they're as cold and hard as they were that first night he showed up here and one look has me pulling my coat closer around me.

"I'm sorry I didn't call you back," I whisper, hating what I'm about to do and the way I've done everything up to this point.

"I know." He takes a long breath and lowers his big body onto the top stair. Knees wide, hands hanging in a loose fold between them, he waits until I sit beside him. "You want to tell me what happened?"

What I want is to climb onto his lap and feel his arms tight around me. I want him to tell me not to worry because everything will be okay, that he's got me, and he won't let go.

And my wanting those things is the problem.

Hugging my knees, I tuck my check into my shoulder and meet his eyes.

"I think everything coming to a head with Greg sort of brought what we were doing into perspective. This has gotten too serious for me." I take a breath, trying to keep the dread spooling through my chest from choking me. "It's not what I want."

It's what I practiced saying with George. What sounded right when we came up with it. But now— God, nothing feels right about it at all.

Vaughn's jaw flexes twice, but his eyes stay locked with mine. All the things he lets me see shuttered away and out of reach. I don't want to cry in front of him, but already I can feel the part of me holding the tears at bay beginning to crumble.

"Say something," I plead.

He brushes a few strands of hair from my face, tucking them gently behind my ear. "It's okay." The back of one knuckle softly runs the line of my jaw, making me ache to lean closer. "You don't date hockey players and I don't date period, right?"

The words are from that first night in Vancouver. Issued between the breathless, desperate kisses that started all this. And now he's bringing them back. Not cruelly. Without animosity.

I nod, and that brutal eye contact slips away, leaving me cold without it.

Pushing to his feet, Vaughn slides his hands into his pockets and starts toward the street. "Take care, Natalie."

Vaughn

I PLUG in my headphones and blast the volume before walking into the locker room the next afternoon.

My *don't fuck with me* vibe must be strong today because everyone keeps their distance as I gear up for practice.

Good. Leave me alone.

It's what I need. What I want.

Let me get through the next months so I can get the fuck out of this city, this state… And never see her again.

Don't think about it.

Never hear her laugh.

Don't.

Never taste her kiss.

The flat of my hand meets the back of my stall and I drag a ragged breath in through my nose.

Calm. The fuck. Down.

It was only a matter of time before it ended. I knew it from the start.

Except, this thing I thought I was prepared for feels like my chest has been ripped open and all the vital organs removed… but somehow I'm still fucking walking around, still expected to function like a living human being. Still expected to perform. To deliver.

Hell, at least that part I can do.

Easing my hand off the wall, I turn to go to practice—and find Baxter six feet away, arms crossed over his chest, an all-too-smug smirk on his face as he watches me. A beat passes and then finally I give him a jut of my chin because I don't have anything else.

His brows buckle, and I head for the ice.

It's the one place where I can shut out the noise. Where there's a single job to do and no room for anything else.

It's what I need.

So I push it, carving up the ice, demanding more drills until Coach forces me to go home.

O'Brian blows up my phone for a while, and I get a message from Garcia, but I don't want to talk. I just want to get through the hours until the next game so I can shut it off again.

Eat.

Sleep.

Skate.

Repeat.

It's a solid plan. At least it seems that way until I come out of the tunnel the next night. Wagner Arena is packed. Lights flashing, music blaring. My eyes zero in on Baxter's seats.

Natalie ought to be filling one. Smiling wide while she waits for her favorite fucking game to start. She ought to be laughing, looking carefree, so I can see for myself that this was the right thing. That she's better off. And then maybe I can let her go.

Only that can't happen because there are a couple of balding, middle-aged fucks occupying the space where she's supposed to be.

———

Natalie

I'M PERCHED at the very edge of my chair, remote clutched against my chest, still barely able to breathe as the commentators continue to discuss Vaughn's game tonight using words like *astounding*, *unprecedented*, and *terrifying*.

The last, in my opinion, being the most accurate.

He was like a man on fire. Relentless. Laser sharp. Almost unnatural.

And with every goal he scored, the look he leveled at the camera following him past the bench was downright chilling. I didn't need the announcer comparing it to the almost playful winks he was throwing out a few weeks prior. I couldn't miss the difference if I tried, and something tells me he knew I wouldn't.

A text alert comes up and I know it's him.

Vaughn: I'm a big fucking boy. Don't skip the games.

I stare at my phone, waiting to see if he'll send anything else. And when it's clear he isn't going to, all that held breath leaks out on a cold laugh as I slump back into the overstuffed chair behind me.

He thinks I didn't go to the game because I was worried *he* couldn't handle it?

I laugh again. And then the tears start to fall, and I turn off the TV and lock up the house because no one is coming over.

———

TWO WEEKS LATER, I've made it to four of the five home games. There haven't been any more texts. The only communication between us comes in that first lap when he skates out onto the ice. His eyes flick to mine as he skates by, and he gives me the slightest nod.

And with Helene holding my hand, I smile like my heart isn't breaking a little more every time I see him. Like I don't think about him every night when I'm going to bed and he isn't on my mind before I even open my eyes in the morning. Like I don't spend half my days wondering when it will stop feeling like this and the other half asking myself if I've made the worst decision of my life.

After the third week, I've stopped crying. Mostly.

I signed up to do a fall-prevention class for the elderly at the community center and picked up a few hours as a trainer for a girls varsity hockey team. I'm staying busy.

Sean is off injured reserve. The guys have one of their longest road trips of the season, so at least I'm not counting down the minutes to some abbreviated head nod wondering if this will be the night I don't get it. Vaughn's game is as intense as ever, smart and focused. And the reporters haven't asked about the rift between him and Greg in weeks. All they want to know is what he's thinking about their chances at the Cup.

By the end of the fourth week, the guys are back. They've had the last two days off and everyone is talking about tonight's game against the Epics. Last time Vaughn faced off against his old team, it was clear there wasn't any love lost between them and there had been a revolving door on the penalty box for both teams.

Vaughn can handle himself, but this game's got me anxious. And to make matters worse, there was some production emergency that had Julia flying out to LA an hour ago, and Helene is babysitting for her cousin. So unless I can find someone to come with me I'll be watching alone. Which is why I'm cutting down the DePaul University neighborhood sidewalk congested with students and early commuters, crossing my fingers that George has a free night. Or at least a night she might be able to free up for me. She's on a very short list of people who understand why I might be particularly invested in a certain grouchy player when I shouldn't be paying attention to him at all.

An old-fashioned bell rings overhead when I walk through The Bike Shop's front door. The walls are exposed brick lined with oversized shelves to accommodate rows of bikes ranging from something a kid would get for her birthday to racing bikes that cost more than George's car. It's early March but there are still a few customers waiting up at the front counter, one with a frame over his shoulder and a wheel that's nearly bent in half in his left hand. Ouch.

George's middle brother, Eli, glances up from the register as his customer signs for his purchase with his finger. "Yo, sis, gonna need you to cover the front." His eyes twinkle with mischief as they meet mine. "My date just got here."

This guy.

"How's it going, Eli?" I ask as George pops up from the bike she's working on in the back. While the front of the store is bright with a clean, sleek style—light pine floors with a dark weather runner leading from the door to the modern counter, high ceilings with recessed lighting—the service area is old-school concrete, bulbs hanging from wires and walls so thick with equipment, I couldn't tell you if they're brick or not. And of course, Awolnation blasting out of a portable speaker with as much grease on it as its owner.

"You wish." George laughs, throwing an elbow into her brother's ribs as she rounds the counter, pulling a dirty rag from her back pocket to wipe her hands.

Eli flashes me a wink. "For about ten years. Nat, when you going to throw me a bone?"

Mmm. That would be a firm never. Eli's a fun guy, but not one you want to date… or let any of your friends date either.

George is wearing a Nirvana T-shirt and has the longer fall of her pixie-cut bangs pinned back from her eyes. She's cute as hell in a totally careless way and even with her brother being within ten feet, two of the guys in line are openly staring at her.

"Hey girl, what brings you over to my little neck of the woods?" she asks me, flashing a warm smile at the customer on his way out.

"Julia had to bail on tonight's game against the Epics. I know you probably have four cousins with birthdays, a great aunt celebrating retirement, and two baptisms—" She rolls her eyes with a laugh, but I'm probably not that far off. George has one of those enormous families that all live within a ten-mile radius and *love* hanging out. "But is there any way you can come with me to the game?" That awesome, bright-as-the-sun smile dims, so I hold up a hand. "The game. That's it. No Five Hole after. Promise."

She bites her lip, thinking it through.

"I'm supposed to help my Aunt Lydia move into her apartment. But there are like fifteen of us planning to go over. She won't mind if I come by tomorrow instead. And if you want to go out with Rux and Greg after, don't skip on my account. One of them can give you a ride and I'll head out after the game."

"I'm not up for hanging out with the team," I say with a look I don't need to explain.

Mouth pulled to the side, she nods. Then after

grumbling something about the players ruining a perfect game, she grabs my hand.

"Come on upstairs with me so I can clean up, and then we can go." We head toward the back of the shop to the stairwell that accesses the apartment she shares with her brothers. "Eli, you're in charge while I'm gone but don't even think about touching that Cannondale I've got on the rack."

"Wouldn't dream of it," he calls back, and then just before we hit the stairs, he adds, "No such promises about Nat, though!"

THE GAME IS ROUGH, the contact charged and excessive. Vaughn's been in the box once already and Rux twice. The Epics are a solid team, but they've got a few guys—like Daryl Hoffman and Rick Gunther—looking for trouble and somehow managing to avoid the worst of the calls. It's getting heated, and I'm glad I've got George beside me for this one.

Flying out of her seat, she bellows, "Cheap shot, Gunther, you Epic *douchebag*! And where's the call, huh? Get your eyes checked, Montgomery!"

George is exactly the kind of distraction I need.

She had a beer in my hand before we sat down and when Vaughn skated past for that first lap, giving me the subtle nod I'd been agonizing over whether I'd see, she gave my hand a squeeze and started talking about the time in college when half the girls on our team got some stomach bug before a bus trip.

But nothing can distract me from the escalating tension on the ice by the third period. The game's 2-2 and Hoffman has been getting into it with everyone. He and Vaughn almost came to blows at the end of the second, and now he's tied up with Greg, helmet to helmet. The whistle blows, and Greg shoves him off, turning to skate away—as Hoffman throws the first punch.

Vaughn

THE SWING IS BULLSHIT, glancing off Baxter's pads and barely budging the guy. Hoffman's an asshole with a short fuse and a grudge against most everyone in the league. He scores like a motherfucker, but he doesn't have the sense to know when to back down. Case in point, the fact that he's still coming after Baxter with Ruxton Meyers closing in fast.

My pulse jacks. Everyone can feel what's coming.

Another shove at Baxter's back, but this time the guy doesn't let it go. Rounding on Hoffman, Baxter shoves the guy, calling him a pussy while Rux holds off another Epics player.

Natalie's up, hands clenched together. Worry etched across her face because this is a volatile mix. But Baxter is a fucking smart player. He's not going to let some shithead goad him into a fight that could get him a turn in the sin bin or worse, tossed from the game. So instead of pushing for the fight brewing in Hoffman's eyes, he gives him a final shove and lines up to face off.

Smart.

The puck drops and it's on. Brutal, intense. Baxter gets control. He's faster than Hoffman, outmaneuvering him at every turn. I see the play open up. Baxter burns down the ice. A flick of the wrist and he wings the puck to Rux for a one-timer into the net. The arena goes wild. But Hoffman isn't done. He flies up behind Baxter, stick raised in both hands as he fucking checks the back of Greg's head into the boards.

What happens next is like a series of stills flashing through my consciousness.

I'm vaulting onto the ice.

My gloves and stick bouncing behind me.

Impact.

Players flooding the ice.

Hoffman rounding on me as I pull him off Baxter. Blood spraying from his mouth when my fist connects.

Impact.

Kneeling beside Baxter as he tries to coordinate his arms and legs to get up. Fails. And goes still.

Panic slicing through me as I find her in the crowd, those big blue eyes wild with fear.

Impact.

Mouthing the words… "*It's going to be okay.*"

Chapter 20

Natalie

"*N*atalie, you've seen him hurt before," George reminds me, rubbing a comforting hand over my arm as we huddle together outside the hospital waiting room. "Concussions are no joke, but your brother has an all-star team of medical professionals behind him. They take this stuff seriously. *He* takes it seriously. He'll do the right things. He'll be careful. And then *he'll be fine*."

I nod. I know she's right. But seeing my big beast of a brother down on the ice like that—*it terrified me*.

Vaughn texted me from the locker room that Greg was awake and already raising hell when they'd loaded him into the ambulance. I spent the drive over getting updates from Julia and passing them on to my mother.

It wasn't until George and I actually got to the hospital that I found out there was another player on his way in.

Vaughn.

He'd shaken off the barrage of punches during the brawl back at the game. I knew he'd been cut, but he seemed okay skating off the ice. And he hadn't mentioned being hurt in his text. But would he?

George groans beside me.

"What?" I look up, but all I see is Quinn O'Brian. He's still wearing his suit from after the game, and he's carrying a couple of coffees our way.

"Hey, Natalie. How's Greg?" he asks, eyes shifting between us as he holds out the steaming paper cups in offering.

I thank him, grateful for the warmth in my hands even if the caffeine is probably a mistake. We talk for a minute about the doctors and what we've both heard, then he turns to George, who's been studiously ignoring him since he walked up. "Don't think we've met before. I'm Quinn."

Her eyes come up, hold for a beat, and then drop back to her phone. "Sure you'd remember if we had?"

What the heck? Okay, yeah, George isn't really into players, but she's never rude. To anyone. But Quinn just shrugs it off with a sheepish grin. "My reputation that bad?"

It is. And any other day, I might tease him about it, but after everything that's happened, I don't have it in me.

George stares at him a moment. Doesn't answer. Then gives my hand a squeeze. "Hey, give me a few minutes to call home before someone decides to track my phone and sees I'm at the hospital."

Quinn watches as she heads down the hall, his eyes lingering in a way that makes me wonder if what she said bothered him more than he let on. But then he clears his throat and gives me an uncertain look.

"What?"

"I'm not sure if this makes a difference, but uhh... Vassar is two doors down from your brother on the right."

Vaughn

THIS IS BULLSHIT. I don't need a fucking hospital.

All I need is an ice bath and a fistful of ibuprofen.

Easing off the hospital bed I don't need to be in, I let out a careful breath and add some tape for my ribs to that list. Yeah, those fuckers are gonna hurt for a couple days, but it's not like I've never played banged-up before.

Baxter's going to be out for a week, minimum. Sean's got heart, but he wasn't a first-line player even before the surgery. And no matter what he says to the press, he's not one hundred percent.

The door opens behind me, and I take another

measured breath, ready to help this doctor see it's time to send me home—except it's not a doctor or a nurse or one of the guys the team sent over.

"Allie."

Those big blue eyes rush over me, taking in the stitches above my ear and on my forearm, the bag of ice wrapped around my knee. I'm glad I'm wearing my sport shorts and a T-shirt instead of one of those gown things that make everyone look frail and fucking weak, because this girl looks like she's had all she can take.

"Are you okay?" she whispers, worry etched in every line of her face and filling her already red-rimmed eyes with tears I don't think I can handle. But then the first one slips past her lashes and—*fuck*—I'm done.

Crossing what's a thankfully small room, I pull her into my side and wrap my arms around her. "I'm fine. Few stitches and a couple bruises. They're just being careful." Ruling out a concussion like Baxter's and any significant damage that would keep me off the ice. "How's your brother?"

A little nod. "He's okay. They're doing some more tests, just to be safe."

I'm glad to hear it. The way Baxter went down tonight—that was rough.

Natalie buries her face against my chest and I can feel her breath over my heart. I shouldn't push it, take more than she means for me to have, but I can't keep my hands from running over her hair and smoothing down her back. I can't keep from touching her like she's still mine.

But if she were mine, I'd be pulling her up onto that shit hospital bed with me and holding her until she felt better.

After a moment, she draws back, but just enough to get a look at me. Her fingers come up to feather over the skin near my stitches. "Does it hurt?"

Yeah, but not the way she's asking. The ache I can't get past is all about her. "Not much."

She nods, and her touch trails lower, whispering over my jaw.

Jesus, that feels good. Too good. I swallow roughly, my hand fisting at the small of her back so I don't slide it into her hair. But she feels it and her eyes come back to mine.

That look. Searching and uncertain. Vulnerable.

Baby, don't look at me like that.

Her thumb skims the edge of my bottom lip, below the split. It's soft and light and I feel it all the fucking way through me. It short-circuits my brain and jump-starts that lifeless organ in the center of my chest.

Catching her hand in mine, I tell myself it's to stop that too-good touch before I do something we'll both regret. Only once my fingers close around hers, the last thing I'm thinking about is pulling her away. Instead I rub my open mouth across the pad of her thumb, the sting from the cut blurring with the heaven of this not-quite-kiss.

Her breath hitches and her lips part. Her eyes dropping to the point of contact between us—to where I'm drawing her hand down to my chest—then climbing back to my mouth as I move closer. Dip lower. Find that spot where our breath meets, warm and wet in a space that's nearly gone.

Knock, knock, knock...

She jerks back from my hold as the dickhead I've been waiting to discharge me comes ambling in, nose in my chart, completely oblivious to the cockblock he just served up. But one look at Natalie's too bright eyes and the way she's hugging her arms around herself like she's afraid she might come apart, and I know I should probably thank the guy.

She wasn't here because she missed me. She was here because she was worried about me. And maybe she needed a little comfort.

Not some dick looking for the first opportunity to take advantage of her.

I know it, and yet I can't make myself look away from her long enough to meet the doctor's eyes, because I'm still hoping I'll see something that tells me I'm wrong. That even though I'm a fucking hockey player and I'm leaving, she wants me anyway.

"Everything looks good, Mr. Vassar. We ought to have you out of here in the next few minutes." He looks over at Natalie, a furrow digging between his brows. "Is this your ride home?"

She shakes her head, backing toward the door. "No, I was just… checking in. I should see if Greg's back. Glad you're okay, Vaughn."

Chapter 21

Vaughn

I'd be an asshole if I wasn't relieved to see Baxter at the practice rink this afternoon.

But I'd be a liar if I said being first line these past two and a half weeks and having a bullshit-free locker room wasn't fucking nice too. No glowers while suiting up. No conversations about Natalie I tell myself I don't need to hear but can't stop listening for. No feeling like an outsider on someone else's team.

Whatever.

It's not like I thought it would last.

I'm coming out of the showers when one of the assistant coaches catches me. The GM wants to talk.

Shit. The last time I got flagged to meet with the GM out of nowhere, I was on a plane to Chicago the next week.

My gut fills with lead as I walk into the locker room still wearing my towel. O'Brian is doubled over watching some YouTube clip on Popov's phone. Rux Meyers, still wearing half his gear, is walking on his hands, bare feet close to the ceiling. A handful of guys give me a nod or hold out a fist for knuckles. And that cold weight inside me doubles with the realization that I'm not fucking ready to leave these guys.

I'm not ready to leave this town, this city… *Natalie.*

That sick feeling starts to spread. My hands feel numb and the noise around me muffles when I think about skating out for the first lap and knowing she's not going to be there. Because I'm in another state. In an arena she may never visit.

She won't be watching me.

She won't be cheering when I score.

She won't be there.

I jam my legs into my track pants and throw on a sport shirt. I need to get upstairs. Stuffing my feet into my gym shoes, I pull out my phone and start scrolling through the sports feeds, because the sad truth is that shit like this gets out. And it's not uncommon to have a trade reported before the player has even been notified. But there's nothing about me beyond a few pictures from the shelter I spent some hours at last week and speculation about whether I'll be starting the next game.

I couldn't give a shit who starts. I just want to know if I'm going to be here.

What if they've got me on a plane tonight?

Will I even get to see her before I leave? Will I even get to say goodbye?

Fuck.

Mateo is outside the general manager's office and waves me through with a clap on my back I can't read.

Raking a hand through my hair, I realize it's still half soaked. Well, it's not like it's going to cost me my spot on the team.

Marty Sheely is wrapping up a call, but signals for me to take a seat in one of the cushy leather chairs across from his desk. He finishes quickly and then leans back, arms crossed over his chest. Sheely is in his mid-forties, pretty fit for a guy who rides a desk, and known to be a straight shooter, so I'm not expecting him to dick me around.

"Vassar, you've been a thorn in my side since the day you arrived. This bullshit with Baxter— Well, we expected some. But we'd hoped you two would be able to put your differences aside for the sake of the organization."

Shit. Did Baxter say something about Natalie? Or fuck, that doctor who walked in? I'd have sworn the guy didn't see anything, and if he had, wouldn't have cared. But—

"And I appreciate that you have."

What?

"Hell, it's no secret this isn't the team you wanted to play for, but you've busted your ass for us. You've contributed to the community as much as any player here. And the way you've stepped up these past few months and especially these last couple weeks hasn't gone unnoticed."

"Thank you, sir."

He levels me with a no-nonsense look. "But Baxter's back this week. And it's his team."

Ah, and now I get it. I was looking a little too comfortable filling the captain's shoes and they want to make sure there won't be any issues with me giving them back.

"He's a good leader." I don't particularly like saying it out loud, but that doesn't make it untrue. "Glad to see him returning to play."

A nod. And then he wags his head and drops an F-bomb under his breath. "I hope Oregon is able to give you what you need when the time comes."

I let out a breath I hadn't realized I was holding. I'm not leaving now.

Which means there's still time.

Though as I'm pushing from the club chair and reaching over the desk to shake his hand, I ask myself, *time for what*?

Natalie's bold and shy smile fills my mind.

"Vassar," he says, stopping me at his door, "it's a shame you and Baxter can't put your personal differences aside, because together you add up to one hell of a team."

I let out a humorless laugh, not because I don't see it, but because I know it's true.

By the time I get back down to the locker room the guys have mostly cleared out. All except the one who hasn't been on the ice in two and a half weeks. He's sitting on the bench, looking like the kid whose mom forgot to pick him up from kindergarten.

I could shove the rest of my gear in my bag and take off. Leave him to his locker room in peace. But instead I sit down and pull out my stick.

"How's the head?" I ask, stripping the tape.

If he's surprised by the question, he doesn't show it. "Better. They're saying I can get back on the ice tomorrow for a no-contact skate. If everything goes right, I'll play Thursday."

"That's good, man. Glad to hear it."

He gives me a disbelieving look, but then shakes his head and sighs. "Thanks. For that, and for what you did with Hoffman. Rux said he was about to throw another punch when you got to him."

I grunt.

He nods.

It's a moment.

One that's blown to hell when I ask, "How's your sister doing?"

His eyes narrow into slits and I hold up a hand, tired of going round with this guy. "I'm not trying to start something. I swear."

"No? So what business is she of yours?"

"I fucking care about her, okay? And since I'm sure the both of you would rather not have me calling her up to see how she's doing, I figure asking you is the lesser evil." My mistake.

But it's got Baxter's attention, because now he's watching me like maybe he's not sure what I'll do if he takes his eyes off me—run off with his sister, maybe.

Or stay for her.

The thought hits me like a club and leaves me reeling. Because it didn't bounce through my consciousness like some internal *ha-ha* joke. It landed like an anvil.

I look at the man eyeing me from across the aisle. There's never been enough room for the both of us. Not in the same room. Not on the same sheet of ice. There's always been too much ego.

And I wonder what would happen if I just... let some of mine go.

Coming in first has been hammered into my head since the first time I put on skates. Anything less was unacceptable. Anything less cost me in ways kids aren't supposed to have to pay.

Being number one meant making the competitive team. It meant making captain. It meant recognition. Opportunity. The right school. The right scholarship. The draft. It meant getting to play instead of going to the farm team. It meant starting. It meant money and endorsements and security.

All the things I've been working toward with an

unwavering commitment from as far back as I can remember. Good things.

But that shit cost me too.

It cost me friends, relationships. It cost me a life.

And now… Christ, could it cost me the only woman who's ever felt like she might be more important than all the rest? Could I have a chance with Natalie if I just let go of being first?

"What the fuck are you looking at me like that for?"

I shake my head. "You ever think about how much shit you had to give up to get here?"

He blinks. "You trying to… *bond* with me right now, Vassar?"

What if instead of seeing Greg Baxter as the guy who is always standing in my way—what if we could see the common ground?

"What if I am?" I let out a rusty laugh at the horrified look on his face and scrub a hand over my jaw. "Don't get your jock in a twist, I'm not talking about moving in on Rux's turf. All I'm saying is, I'm not fifteen years old anymore. We're on the same team and maybe if we stopped to look, I'm betting—"

"Jesus Christ, this is still about Natalie, isn't it?" He shoves to his feet and, yeah, I'm watching for any sign moving that fast rocked him, but the guy looks steady. Steady and pissed. "Vassar, you don't actually think that getting me behind you will give you a better shot, do you? You're *leaving*."

Even as he says it, I'm running the possible plays in my head.

He gapes, going two shades paler in a blink. "Did you fuck up with Oregon?"

"What? No." If anything, Oregon wants me more than ever.

Baxter swallows, his eyes narrowing into the hard scowl we've been exchanging since high school. He stalks closer, pointing at my chest. "Well, don't. And whatever shit you've got spinning in that head about my sister, knock it off. Nat's doing fine. Better than, so do me a favor—screw that, do *yourself* a favor and forget about her."

I'm off the bench, hands flying out to the sides. "You think I haven't tried? I know she thinks it won't work with us…"

"It won't." He shrugs, stepping back, but I'm not done. I don't even care if he's listening.

"And that I can't give her what she needs…"

He drops his head back. "Dude, *you can't.*"

"But I'm starting to think she's wrong. I'm starting to think she's—"

"She's… she's with another guy."

The words knock me back a step, hitting harder than any punch this guy has ever thrown. I try to shake it off, but I feel like I'm the one laid out on the ice, unable to coordinate my limbs to get up. And this time it's Greg fucking Baxter looking down at me with—hell, is that *pity* in his eyes?

"Bullshit." I can barely get the word past my teeth. The last time I was alone with her we almost kissed. And yeah, that was two and a half weeks ago, and she was emotional, scared. But… *fuuuck*.

"It's not."

"Is it serious?" I choke out, hating that I'm talking to her brother about this more than I've ever hated anything in my life.

We were serious. Too serious for what she wanted.

Not serious enough to make it work anyway.

"It's… a recent thing. She wanted to move on. There were a few guys. Successful, local. Not hockey players. She hit it off with one. But… uhh… yeah, it could be serious. They have a lot in common. I know she's seeing him tonight. And hell, I like him."

Baxter's met him already? That burns, but why not. This guy isn't some dirty secret she's trying to keep from everyone, hoping they run their course before people find out.

I fall back onto the bench behind me.

Baxter's hand lands on my shoulder. "Look, man, I know this isn't what you want to hear. But—you don't know what it was like for her growing up. My parents— I don't think they see what they did to her. How they treated her. And I was so caught up in my own shit, I didn't realize until it was too late. But Natalie *never* came first. It was like what happened in her life didn't matter. They didn't go to her games. They didn't take her to the tournaments. They didn't answer the phone when the coaches were calling to tell them she was in the hospital. All they could see was me. My game, my future. It was bullshit, and I'll regret not doing enough to change it when it mattered for the rest of my life. But right now, I can do something for her."

I look up at the guy who's been my biggest rival since I was fifteen years old, not caring that he can see how wrecked I am. "What?"

"I can tell you to leave her alone. Finish out the season and when Oregon offers you that fat contract, take it and go. Give Natalie the chance to have the life she deserves."

Chapter 22

Natalie

"Greg, you sound weird. Did you hit your head again? Does it hurt? Was it too much today? I told you to play it safe and give it another day, no matter what the doctors said. What was one more day?"

"Chill! Jesus, Nat, my head is fine. Relax, okay?" he snaps through the line as I resume running my pitiful little basket of frozen dinners for one through the self-checkout.

"Well, good. Don't scare me like that." One of the protein bowls won't scan so I try to get the attention of the lone clerk a few aisles down. "So what's going on then?"

Because he totally sounds weird.

"Can't a guy ask his sister to meet him for dinner?"

I look down at the box dinner I still can't scan. "Umm, gee Greg, that's really nice of you. But I sort of have other plans."

Which may or may not include bingeing some of Vaughn's old games and a few rounds of *will I, won't I* before finally breaking down and trolling social media and—to my eternal shame—some of the bunny boards for sightings.

I want to know what he's wearing. If he's been hanging out with the guys at the Five Hole.

Closing my eyes, I take a slow breath.

If he's been with anyone else.

It's going to happen. One of these days he's going to stop shooting the women down and I'm going to find a post that will kill me. And I'm going to tell myself I needed to see it. That it's a good thing. Because it means that he's moving on. And then maybe I'll be able to too.

Maybe I'll be able to let him go.

Greg growls through the line. "Nat, for the record I'm pretty sure you don't have any plans at all. But even if you did. Cancel them. Come hang out… I… uhh… Julia's out of town and I need to talk, okay? Meet me at Belfast in twenty minutes."

"Wait, not Belfast—" But he's already gone.

TWENTY MINUTES and one abandoned basket of frozen dinners later, I'm shaking off the spring mist as Brody, Belfast's owner, cuts through the after-work crowd to wrap a burly arm around me.

"Natalie! Greg's got a table in the Back Room. Want me to send over a Goose Island?"

I thank him and head toward the closed-off part of the bar, usually reserved for nights with live music. Greg's sitting at one of the high-tops near the stage, a water and what looks like the remains of a burger plate in front of him. I check the time on my phone. I'm not late.

"Did you *already eat?*" So much for dinner.

"Yeah, I was starving," he says, rubbing a hand over his flat stomach, flashing me a quick grin.

This guy does not look like he has anything heavy weighing on his mind. In fact, he kind of looks delighted with himself.

An uneasy feeling comes over me.

"Greg. What's going on?"

Shoving up from his seat, he waves me into one of the open ones. "Give me a minute. I'll put your order in. Chicken Alfredo?"

"Roadhouse burger with rings."

"Right." He leans in, smacks a kiss on my temple and rubs the top of my head like a dog.

Cripes.

A minute passes. I check my phone.

Another. I pull up Instagram. Start the search of

shame. There's a sighting from two nights ago, where someone caught a picture of Vaughn filling up his car with gas. It's a picture I've looked at too many times already. My thumb hovers over the button. *Hovers, hovers, hovers…*

Finally I take the screen shot and save it to my phone.

"Such a *stalker*," I groan.

What am I doing?

"Hey, Nat?" an unfamiliar guy asks, leaning into my field of vision with a bright smile.

"Yes?" I'm trying to place his face, but not getting any hits. That still doesn't mean we haven't met. I meet a lot people through the clinic, volunteering, and Greg.

He sticks his hand out to shake. "Chad Benson. I'm on Greg's team of financial managers."

"Oh, nice to meet you."

He slides onto the chair to my right, which seems sort of strange and presumptuous until he adds, "Greg said I should join you."

I'm about to say something polite when another guy I don't know pops up beside us. "Natalie, right?" he says, leaning in for some kind of one-armed squeeze that has little alarms sounding in the back of my head. "Dwayne Levine, I'm one of Greg's trainers. Great to meet you. Really great."

What the heck?

He takes the chair to my left. Reaches over the table with a friendly smile to shake with the finance guy.

Then turning back to me, he grins. "So this is fun, huh?"

I crane around, searching for my brother, when a third guy steps past the rope separating us from the main bar.

Three guys I've never met. Nice enough looking. Athletic builds… but not pros.

Number three drops into Greg's seat, ignoring the empty plate there, and gives me a nod and once over that has my jaw dropping as I suck in a horrified breath.

Three guys… who are big-brother approved.

And no brother in sight.

"GREG BAXTER, I don't care if you are concussed or not, you are a *dead man*!" I bellow, storming into my brother's apartment like I own the place. Or like I know it will torque him off if I act like I do.

"Natalie?"

My head swings around to where Julia is sitting on the floor in her living room with her friends Laurel and Margo, and her little sister, Cammy.

"What are you doing here?" I ask, confused because Greg's whole excuse for wanting to hang out was that Julia wasn't in town.

Cammy turns to her sister and, pointing a sloshing martini at her, giggles. "Yeah, Jules, what *the hell* are you doing in your own home? Quick, someone call the cops."

The steel leaves my spine, and I slump into the wall. "Sorry, Julia. Your husband told me—and I thought—" Closing my eyes, I shake my head. "I'm so sorry for crashing in here like a psycho."

"We'll forgive you," Margo offers, waving her own drink around. "But only if you come in and dish the deets on what's got you so hopping mad."

All the girls are nodding, patting the carpet beside them. I let out a long breath and cross to an open spot between Cammy and Margo. I don't really know Margo too well except that she and Laurel go back and I'm pretty sure she has a thing for Laurel's brother, but Cammy and I spent two years together at Bearings High School, and we've become pretty good friends since Julia and Greg got together. She's got the cutest kid on the planet and, when it comes to romance, about as much luck as me.

"Where's the kiddo tonight?" I ask, sinking to the floor and accepting the drink Margo has already mixed for me.

"Rux."

I raise a brow.

"Word to the wise, don't make bets with Julia."

Margo pushes back one of the ebony ringlets spilling out from her headband and clears her throat. "Yeah, that's nice and all, but I'm still waiting to hear about what Greg did."

All eyes light up, and I swear they lean in in unison.

"Oh yeah. Do tell!" Julia beams, scrunching back against the base of the sofa. "He's been so bored cooped up for the past few weeks. I can't wait to hear this."

"Apparently he decided to celebrate his freedom by helping me out with my love life."

Cue the round of *awws* that have me knocking back half my drink. It practically comes back out when the burn hits and, coughing, I gape at Margo.

She shrugs and tops off my glass.

"He what?" Julia looks delighted. Of course she does.

"*No*. You do *not* give me that 'oh, my husband is completely adorable' look," I huff.

"That really is kind of adorable though," Cammy agrees with a sigh. "Did he introduce you to a friend?"

Ha! "Try *three* friends. And to say he introduced us would be a stretch."

Julia's blond brows arch, like maybe she's seeing this isn't quite so cute as she thought. "How's that?"

"Yeah, how's that?" Margo echoes, waving me on. "I want to adjust my expectations before I get too excited about you telling me about some four-way action."

The next gulp goes down smoother. "Sorry, way off, Margo. What he did was ditch me at Belfast and then blindside me with not one, not two, but three different blind dates that apparently all had his stamp of approval."

"What?" Julia coughs, pushing up to her knees. "Not all at once though?"

"Oh yeah. One, two, three. A nice little square table with me on one side and the three of them around the others. All shaking hands with each other. Complimenting me on my Wisconsin hoodie with a hole in the shoulder."

Laurel's outraged on my behalf, but I'm getting the sense it's got more to do with being underdressed for three first impressions. Margo wants to know if I picked one and whether we hooked up. And Julia, cripes, she's muttering something about how such a sweet, smart guy could be so dense… looking like she *still* finds it completely adorable.

How is it that I'm the only one pissed about this?

Except, I know someone else who would be equally enraged… probably even more so. But telling *him* would be a serious mistake. One, because we aren't together anymore. And two, because Vaughn losing his shit with so much riding on his good behavior would be a disaster. He needs to get away from Greg, not end up brawling with him in the street.

So even though he might be the only person capable of understanding how much this bothers me, I can't talk to him about it.

I can't talk to him about anything.

My chest feels tight, and there's a burn in the back

of my throat that has nothing to do with Margo's napalm-strength drink. It's Vaughn. I miss him and it hurts. So stupid. He's potentially the worst guy I could pick in the non-criminal, STD-free universe. I knew it in Vancouver.

Before that.

I've known it since he was that hothead at the tournaments. But even so, I let myself get attached. I let myself fall for him.

God, I let myself love him.

With an unsteady hand, I hold out my glass for a refill.

"Whoa, ladies," Margo cuts in, setting my glass aside and then rubbing my arm gently. "Natalie doesn't look so good."

"I'm fine." I shake my head, but the tears are already in my eyes, dang it. "Frustrated after today is all."

Suddenly, everyone is sitting closer. Julia takes my hand in hers. "Hey, I get it. Greg can be… a little pushy and overbearing when he gets something in his head. He doesn't know how to quit. But I mean, look on the bright side, you had dinner with three guys decent enough your brother actually likes them, and enamored with you enough to go on a… three-way blind date."

"Four-way." Margo looks around. "Right?"

"Okay, a four-way." Her eyes light up and she gives my hand a squeeze. "Even better."

They have no idea. And how would they, never

having to figure out the hard way that the guy giving you all his attention is more interested in your brother than you. Those guys tonight hadn't even met me before. They have no reason to want to date me. But because my brother asked them to, they not only met me for a blind date, but they willingly went into it knowing they'd be with two other guys. Give me a break. That's not about me.

That's about Greg.

And for as much as I know these girls care about me, I'm pretty sure they can't really see past my brother either. Julia, she shouldn't have to. Cammy has had a case of Greg worship since high school. Laurel wasn't that close to Greg in high school, but her husband Jack was. And Margo… well, she's… awesome, but maybe a little nutty and probably Team Greg like everyone else.

And why shouldn't they be? He's a great guy.

It's just not so great being his sister sometimes.

Besides, the way I'm feeling isn't really about this latest example of why it's hard for me to trust the motives of the guys who ask me out. It's about Vaughn, the guy I need to let go.

Margo presses a full glass back into my hand and holds up her own.

"Okay, so let's get to the good stuff. There are three guys, which one are you keeping and which ones do Cammy and I get?"

It's easy to get pulled into the laughter with these girls, and soon enough, we're ordering Thai food and cheesecakes. When Rux calls for my wuss brother—who is apparently back at Cammy's place helping babysit—to find out how mad I am on a scale of walking into my room without knocking to breaking my new stick before the championship game at State… I hand my phone off to Margo. I didn't realize she and Rux knew each other, but she's laughing within seconds and asking him about *his* stick while Laurel and Cammy chime in from the background. Pretty sure the stick in question is *not* the one that got him the assist two days ago against the Blues.

Gross.

Pushing up from the floor, I head into my brother's ultra-modern kitchen and pour myself a tall glass of water. The lights are off and it's kind of nice to just stand here in the dark looking out over the sparkling cityscape.

"Hey, how you doing?" Julia asks, coming up beside me.

"Better than I was." I hand her the glass I poured and fill another for myself. "Your husband is on my shit list, no question. But I'm prepared to let him live."

She snorts, and it's so at odds with the perfection of her classic beauty, I can't help but laugh.

"Well, I appreciate it."

I sigh, turning to her. "Sorry for barging in like a lunatic, but thank you for letting me stay. I needed a night like this more than I realized."

Nodding toward the front room, she smiles.

"There's no one better than these girls. And I'm glad you stayed. I miss seeing you laugh."

I give her a wan smile, but what can I say?

"Have you talked to him lately? Vaughn?"

I close my eyes, wondering how I can be surprised that Julia knows. "Greg told you?"

"Yeah, but I'd already figured it out." Of course she had. It's what she does. "Sorry I called him an asshole."

Cutting her a look, I let out a chuckle. And when she holds out an arm, I don't fight it. I take the hug I kind of desperately need and hold on. "He slugged your husband. You were entitled."

She wants to know about Vancouver and what it was like when he first figured out who I was. I tell her about those early nights of fighting what quickly began to feel inevitable, and for a minute it feels like I'm there again, on the brink of something amazing. Something that feels so right…

Covering my eyes, I say what I've been trying to deny for too long. "I think I made a mistake."

Chapter 23

I should get the fuck out of here. Not a news flash. I've been telling myself the same thing since I pulled up to Natalie's place and started loitering on her stoop like a damn vagrant. No, not a vagrant—*a stalker*.

She's got a date tonight.

A date with someone who could be serious. A guy Baxter likes and approves of. Someone she likes enough to be out with until two thirty in the morning.

Jesus.

Dates don't last that long if they aren't going well. If there isn't something there. And even if there is, most restaurants, movies and bars aren't open this late. My gut knots, and for a minute I can't breathe. Because if she isn't at any of those places and she isn't here, then she went home with him.

I should go. Only there's no fucking way I will. Not until I see with my own eyes that he's better for her than I am.

Headlights slice through the darkness and I wait like I have the past dozen times, hoping it's her, hating him.

The car stops at the curb—*a limo*—and my knuckles crack as I pray this cheesy, pretentious fuck doesn't try to kiss her good night. That she doesn't invite him in. I don't even want to know what he looks like, what his name is, or how I could find him when I think about his hands on her. His mouth. *Motherfucker*, anything else.

But I have to.

The car door opens and I hear her laugh. It's not something I'm prepared for and for a minute I think I might puke.

Then she's stepping out of the car. Make that *stumbling* out of the car and laughing some more.

That fucker got her drunk?

My feet start to move. He's dead. And if I don't get to finish the job before the cops arrive, it's a safe bet Baxter will do it himself when he hears.

And what the hell? He isn't even getting out to walk her to her door?

I'm ready to take this guy's head off—except then I'm not, because Natalie looks up and our eyes meet and suddenly it's just her and me and this thing between us I can't explain. Her laughter fades and her smile softens, spreading as she starts walking toward me through the grass. The look in her eyes is the one I see in my dreams and has me forgetting about the guy, the car, about anything beyond her.

She doesn't stop until we come together. Her finger-tips making first contact at my ribs, her palms pressing in a heartbeat later as she slides her hands up my chest and around my neck.

"You're here," she whispers, eyes shining bright. "I wanted you to be here… and you are."

"Allie," I growl, heart slamming as my arms come around her waist. "Baby, are you okay?"

She nods, her fingers sifting through the hair at the back of my neck. "I think I might be now." And then she does it, goes to her toes and pulls me down into her kiss.

"Christ, I've missed you," I say against her lips, not willing to break the contact. Not willing to risk this moment.

She nods against my mouth, and I feel the quake in her body before I taste the salt on her lips.

"Tears?" I choke, searching her watery eyes before looking back to the limo.

But instead of finding some douche I need to murder, it's Baxter's wife in the open door. And she's waving at us with a big smile while the other three girls filling the space around her stare, mouths gaping wide.

Girls. That's who she was out with after hours.

I raise a hand to them in a half wave acknowledging

that I've got her, and then my focus is back on Natalie. When we get inside, I drop onto the couch and pull her into my lap. "Why are you crying?"

Another tear slips down her cheek and the smile she gives me breaks something inside me I didn't know I had.

"I did something stupid, Vaughn." Her words are a whisper and she can't look at me.

Is she talking about her date?

I can barely breathe through the raw pain in my chest. I never should have let her go. But it's not too late, because she's not cuddled up in his bed. She's here with *me*. Her fingers are wrapped in *my* shirt. And *I'm* the one she kissed.

I cup her cheek in my palm and bring those tragic blue eyes back to mine, so she can see that I mean what I'm about to say. "Whatever it is, it doesn't matter. If you need to tell me, I'll listen. But it won't change anything. Do you understand?"

Her chin starts to quiver, and I can't take it. "Allie, you're killing me."

Eyes locked with mine, she slowly shakes her head. "I didn't mean to do it. I knew better, but somehow… I fell in love with you anyway."

The chaos that's been tearing through my mind comes to a stop. "What?"

I heard her wrong. She said she did something stupid. She was out with some guy. She—

"I'm in love with you," she whispers again. "I know

it's not what we talked about. I know we aren't together anymore, and if you don't feel the same way it's okay, but I don't—"

My mouth comes down over hers in a crush and I kiss her like she's the air I need to breathe. Like I'm never going to let her go. And then she's shifting in my arms, pressing her sweet curves into me, fisting her hands in my hair.

God, I fucking love that. I love the tug just sharp enough to tell me this isn't some dream. It's real. It's not over. She doesn't belong to someone else.

I'm devouring her. She tastes like tears and sugary cocktails and *Allie*, and I can't get enough.

Except then that particular flavor combination registers and I realize it's going to have to be enough. Because I don't know how much she's had to drink, which means I don't know how she's going to feel about this tomorrow.

I love you…

I don't know if it's how she really feels or if it's how she feels *right now*.

Drawing back, I press my forehead against hers and take a slow breath. She dips her head, seeking more of my kiss. I give it to her, but softly.

"Allie, baby, we need to slow down."

She shakes her head, coming back for another kiss it nearly kills me to cut short.

Stroking her cheek, I meet her eyes. "I want you more than I've ever wanted anything in my life. But not like this. Not when there's a chance you'll regret it tomorrow."

"Nooo," she says in this whimpering voice that's so fucking cute, I can't help but laugh. "I'm not drunk. Okay, I'm a little drunk. Do you know Margo?"

I smooth the hair from her face, tucking it behind her ear. "No, I don't think so."

"She makes *really* good drinks."

"Yeah?" Adjusting her in my arms, I push up and carry her toward her bedroom. "Maybe I'll get to try one sometime."

"After you win the Cup," she murmurs, resting her head on my shoulder. I can feel her body going lax. "Before you leave."

I can't think about that right now.

She presses her hand over my heart. "Before *we* leave. Imma come too."

I almost trip carrying her. But I get my shit together and, holding her closer, carry her to her bed. "We can talk about that tomorrow."

I set her down and help her with her shoes and socks. Her sweatshirt. Damn, I love her in this sweat-shirt. My little jock.

"Will you stay with me?" Her eyes are sleepy but pleading. "I haven't been sleeping so good lately."

Me either. "Yeah, sweetheart, I'll stay."

Chapter 24

Natalie

*M*y bed is empty.

He was here when I got home last night. Waiting for me. I told him I loved him… and he stayed. I fell asleep to the steady beat of his heart and the heat of his big body wrapped around me. But now that spot where he was is empty and—

"Morning."

I gasp, twisting around.

Vaughn's sitting in the chair in the corner of my room, chin resting on his fists. He's wearing his jeans and a fitted, deep vee T-shirt, and as incredibly hot as that is, he looks exhausted.

"I thought you were gone." I sit up and see that I'm wearing a sleep tank and *panties*. Not what I went to bed in.

"You got hot," he croaks out, his eyes locked on the sheet covering what I'm guessing is the reason he's over there instead of still in bed with me.

And yeah, I've got a fuzzy memory of stumbling around kicking off my jeans and T-shirt. Losing my bra. And then crawling back into bed.

"Umm… How long have you been in that chair?"

"Few hours." He swallows, the thick muscles of his neck working up and down. "You're wearing my number."

The panties with Vaughn's number on them. The ones that drove him *insane* the night I wore them, the night everything fell apart.

"I'm a fan?" I offer weakly, heat pushing into my cheeks, because I really didn't think he'd see them. I was just missing him and, silly as it was, they made me feel a little bit better.

Rubbing his big hand over his jaw, he nods. "A fan, huh? You still feel that way this morning?"

I nod. Glad for the opening, but still nervous. What if he doesn't want what I want… or at least not all of it?

Only one way to find out.

"I do." I think I might feel that way for the rest of my life. "Vaughn, I—I made a mistake. Everything with you was so much more than I expected. More than I kept telling myself I could have. But I wanted it. I wanted you. I just got—"

"Scared." No judgment, only the gruff acknowledgement that he understands. More evidence that this man deserves more credit than I've given him. But that's been my problem from the start.

"I was so afraid of what being with you might mean —what I thought it would cost me—I couldn't see what was right in front of me, what it was *actually like*. The ways you've been putting me first, showing me that I matter, from the very beginning." I look away, blinking back the emotion filling my eyes. I pushed him away. I hurt him. "You've never once made me feel like an afterthought. Or that what was happening in my life didn't count. You watched my games and remembered my friends' names when you hadn't even met them. You held me when I was scared and let me go when I thought it was what I needed... But Vaughn, it's not what I need. I love you and I'm asking you to give me another chance. To let me be there for you the way you're there for me."

He takes a deep breath, and I get the sense he's holding himself back. "Natalie, you're asking *me* for another chance?" Running his hand down his face, he shakes his head. "I'd give you anything you want. But what are we talking about here? The next few months or—fuck, baby, please tell me you're talking about longer."

Crawling out of bed, I move to his lap. His eyes flick to my panties and he bites his lip, but instead of reaching for me, he fists his hands and leans back to make room for me against his chest.

I stroke his jaw, loving the coarseness against my

fingertips. The ways he's rough around the edges in some ways and so soft in others. "I'm talking about where you go, I go… If that's what you want?"

Chapter 25

Vaughn

*I*f *that's what I want?*

She has to ask?

I'm off the chair in a heartbeat and then Natalie's back on her bed with me following her down. "Baby, I'm going to show you what I want…"

Eyes wide, lips parted on a pretty little gasp, she's sexy as fuck. "I want you any way I can have you…"

She could have skipped that whole amazing speech, shot me a glance over her shoulder and said, "Okay." And I'd have been all in, knowing that I was the luckiest guy on the planet.

I grab my T-shirt and pull it off. "I want you in every way…"

"You do?" she gasps, wiggling beneath me to get her tank top off.

"Oh yeah." Christ, her tits are perfect. Her tight little nipples sweet on my tongue. "But not for a few months…"

I've got my fly open, and she's using her feet to help push my jeans and boxer briefs down. "How long?"

Forever.

"Not a couple weeks…" Kicking them free, I back off the bed far enough to get a look at her hot-as-fuck panties. I almost creamed myself when she got up last night and started shimmying out of her clothes. Bending over and—God help me—flashing my number stitched across her ass like a claim.

Carefully, carefully, I inch them down her thighs and off her feet. Then, pushing her knees apart, I move into the space between.

Her knees slide up my sides, one pretty foot hooking against my thigh while the other climbs higher. Her skin is like silk.

Pulling back, I position my cock so it's notched against her. I'm propped on my forearms by her head. I want to see her eyes while I love her. I want her to see mine. "I'm never going to let you go."

A tear slips from the corner of her eye as she smiles up at me. "I'm yours."

"Mine." Saying it calls to a primal part of me, and I can't wait anymore.

I've had her hard and fast, I've had her desperate and needy, I've had her against nearly every wall and horizontal surface her place has to offer, but I've never had her like this. I've never had her when I was as deep in her heart as I was in her body, and I want it to last.

I sink into her slick heat, savoring every inch I claim, every soft gasp and tight clench. When I'm as deep as I can be, our fingers thread together over her head. I'm still swimming in the sea of her eyes when I start to move. Pulling back as slowly as I sank in and then doing it again.

"Tell me. Baby, I need to hear it again."

"I love you," she whispers.

"Christ, you don't know what hearing you say that does to me. How much it means." I'm not the best. I'm not first. I've fucked up every step of the way. But she loves me anyway.

Rocking into her, I push her toward release. I work my body for hers until I feel the clench of her around me, the catch of her breath, and the tightening of her fingers with mine.

"Allie." She's coming apart, but our eyes are still locked together. I don't want to lose the contact. Not before I tell her. "*Natalie*, baby, I love you."

I've never said it before. The words should have felt clumsy in my mouth, but they felt like they belonged there. More right than firing a puck that hits dead center. So right, I need to say them again.

"I love you." I say it for her. Low and fierce. Rough and deep. I whisper it against her mouth and growl it against her neck. I swear it as she shatters to my confession. Her body gripping mine with rhythmic pulses, my name on her lips and my heart in her hands.

Natalie

IT'S a good thing Vaughn has a late practice, because I'm not ready to let him go.

We've been lazing in bed, touching, breathing each other in. I fan my fingertips over the rough stubble of his jaw and brush my thumb against his lips.

This man has the most perfect mouth in all the land.

Catching my thumb between his teeth, he gives it a quick nip and then a slow suck. He groans and, gripping my ass, pulls me over his hard-on.

A thought comes to me and I press a hand against his chest.

He raises a brow.

"Hey, I never asked, but what were you doing here last night?"

His nostrils flare as he blows out a breath before meeting my eyes. "Your fucking brother told me about your date and I kind of lost it."

Greg must have a death wish or something, because the look on Vaughn's face even now, with me lying naked on top of him, is not a comforting one. "Is he—"

"He's fine. I told you I wouldn't mess with him, even if the guy can't stop messing with me."

Wait— "He told *you*, but he didn't have the balls to tell me?"

Vaughn's chin jerks back, his brows furrowing deep. "What the hell does that mean?"

I explain about the night before and when I'm through, Vaughn pushes the sexed-up, messy morning curls from my face and searches my eyes. He gets it.

"The second I saw you in Vancouver I started warning guys off with looks that promised death. I would never have sat there with two other guys."

"You would have left?"

The scoff he lets out says no. "I would have thrown you over my shoulder like a caveman and carried you out."

"Aww, you say the sweetest things." I mean it.

Hands coasting over my hips, he asks, "So what happened?"

"I went to Greg's apartment to tear him a new one, but Julia was having a girls' night, so I stayed instead."

He starts to smile. "And that's how you ended up stumbling in after two a.m. with a limo full of girls."

"They didn't want me to have to take a car alone and Julia probably didn't totally trust me not to hunt down her husband and maim him." I bite my lip, meeting his eyes. "But what were you doing here… after two a.m. when you thought I was out on a date?"

"Fighting for you… but trying to fight fair."

Butterflies stir up in my belly and my voice is a little breathy when I ask what he means.

Vaughn raises his arms and scrubs his hands through his hair. "I mean, I've been going fucking nuts without you. And the idea of another man taking you out, doing the things we haven't done or worse, the things we have… I could barely handle it. Your brother told me you'd met someone and it might be serious."

What!? Oh, Greg is a dead man.

Only Vaughn's not done. "I thought… if I saw you with him… if you looked happy, really happy… I might be able to let you go."

And with this those few words I forget about Greg and let go of the righteous pissed building inside me… because this is what matters. This minute. This man.

My heart feels too full and my lungs too weak. "Because you wanted me to be happy?"

That steady gray stare doesn't waver. "More than my next breath."

I love him.

"And if I *hadn't* looked happy? What would you have done then?" I ask softly, but the answer is right there in his eyes.

"Then I would have been waiting at your door when he walked you up. I would have told him, sorry, but he was out of luck." He drags his bottom lip through his teeth, and I squirm a little. "And then I would have had you moaning my name against that door before he got back to his car."

"You wouldn't even wait until he was gone?" I whisper.

"Baby, I wouldn't even wait until we were *inside*." Heat rushes through me, because he's serious. Sliding his fingers into the hair at the back of my neck, he strokes his thumb over the line of my jaw. "Natalie, if I'd thought that was my chance, I wouldn't have waited a single second."

Vaughn

BAXTER GIVES me a wide berth when I show up to practice. But even fresh off a concussion, I can see he's bristling, ready for a fight. *Fucker.*

Lucky for him, I've promised my girl I wouldn't take him apart limb from limb.

There is zero chance he doesn't know about last night. His wife was in the car watching when Natalie laid that kiss on me. And I'm pretty sure she and her friends were all still gawking when we went into her place together.

Everyone's getting their equipment on and filing out of the locker room, but Baxter hangs back. Rux cuts a look my way and shakes his head, leaving us alone.

I cross my arms and jut my chin at him. "Something on your mind?"

Like that fucked-up date you sent your sister on last night? Or how you lied about her being in a new relationship?

"I thought you let her go."

I left her alone for close to two miserable months. And it nearly broke us both. "Yeah? I thought Natalie was seriously stoked about her date—*dates?*—last night. Looks like we were both wrong." I pinch the bridge of my nose and then shoot him a hard glare. "You have any idea how shitty you made her feel?"

He rolls his eyes and blows out a pissy breath. "I thought she'd—"

"You thought she'd come after you, which is why you pulled the pussy move and snuck out of Belfast without bothering to make sure she was okay with what you'd done. You didn't even make sure she got home okay. Small fucking wonder she's got so many issues about being with a player."

He coughs, hands coming up beside him. "I was giving her some time to cool off. And those were damn decent guys I picked for her. Short fucking notice too."

It clicks. This was about him warning me off. He lied to me and then tried to make it the truth.

"You dumb fuck. You know what she saw? More assholes willing to jump through outrageous hoops for you. Not her. *You.*"

"That's not how it was. These guys have tickets to anything they want to see. They work in one way or another with players all the time."

"Yeah, but that's not the same as being a part of

your actual life. Being your brother-in-law. Seriously, man. Some dude asks you to play the dating game with his sister… sit there with two other dudes and let her pick… you going to do that?"

He gets that belligerent look in his eyes I think is so hot on his sister and I want to sock him in the teeth for ruining something I fucking love.

"No, but I'm married."

I don't have time for this shit. Grabbing my stick and helmet, I start for the ice.

"Fine," he grunts from behind me. "I fucked up."

"Don't tell me, dickhead. Tell Natalie. Make it up to her."

I'm halfway through the door when he calls after me. "How?"

I could keep going. Pretend I don't hear him. But what's that going to do for any of us? Nothing I want. So I turn around, ready to let some of that ego go. "Actually, I've got an idea. And you're *really* not going to like it… but your sister will."

Chapter 26

Natalie

*W*e made it to conference finals, but lost game seven in double overtime. Greg blamed me for jinxing the team by wearing Vaughn's jersey instead of his. No one took him seriously because I'd worn it to all the other playoff games we won, but he didn't drop it until I mentioned how very lucky *I* got wearing those numbers.

Mean? Maybe. But Big Brother had it coming.

Fortunately, the team and management took the news about Vaughn and my relationship pretty well. It helped that Julia broke the story during an interview with Vaughn after a round-one playoff win when, in addition to two assists, my man scored the winning goal. Greg obviously knew about the interview ahead of time and was a good sport about the whole thing, even making a scowly cameo appearance so funny, the clip went viral.

The two guys have been flooded with interview requests ever since, but neither seems too keen on accepting. There'll be plenty of interviews when Vaughn's new contract goes through. Oregon wants him bad and their offer shows it.

Nothing's official yet, but at this point, it could be any minute.

"Hey, babe, you ready to head over to my place?" Vaughn asks, coming up behind me to kiss my neck.

Setting my empty mug in the sink, I snuggle into his hold. "You bet."

I thought I'd hold on to some doubts or reservations about what our relationship would mean for my life, but every time I think about our future together, all I feel is this joyful sense of relief. Like suddenly this kind of critical thing I didn't even realize I was missing is right where it's supposed to be.

Yeah, there are still a lot of unknowns ahead, but the one thing I do know is that I love this man and my life is infinitely better with him than it could ever be without.

"Got a bag?" he asks, taking my hand as we walk through my place.

"Front hall." We don't spend as many nights here these days. Security is better at his place, but last night he got sentimental and wanted to stay here. Or more specifically he wanted to do me against the door and then stay here.

Honestly, he has some really good ideas.

And since we were here, I figured I'd grab a few more things. We basically live together, but since we'll be moving at the start of next season, it didn't really make sense to pack more than once. And this works fine for now.

Vaughn swings my bag over his shoulder and, fingers caught in a loose hold, we head out.

It's after noon on a sunny warm Saturday and it still tickles me a little that we can leave my place without worrying who's going to see us these days. There's usually someone. A reporter parked down the block or sometimes just a Slayers fan out for a walk. What's weird though is that so many of them recognize me too, calling out our names like we're friends when I've never laid eyes on them before.

That I haven't gotten used to.

The trip from my place to Vaughn's isn't far. We drive through familiar neighborhoods, passing favorite stores and hangouts. I'm going to miss this town. I'll be back for visits, but it won't be the same.

And I'm okay with that.

All those months ago, I told Vaughn I was afraid of not having a choice about what my life looked like. And every day I thank my stars that I do. That I got to choose what mattered to me most. *That I got to choose him.*

The rest will come. A job. Coaching. Friends. Community. It's going to be different than it was when I was a kid. Vaughn asked me to trust that he'd make sure it was, and I do. Completely.

He pulls down the alley and punches in the security code for the garage to park.

I climb out the passenger side and look through the small window toward the house. "I know we talked about waiting until closer to the season start to move, but maybe we should do it sooner."

He raises a brow from across the hood. "Yeah?"

I shrug. "Give ourselves a chance to settle in before things get too intense from your end. I don't know, do something crazy like actually decorate."

"I like the idea of decorating." He holds out his arm, waiting for me to tuck myself in for the walk through the breezeway to the house. "Playing with that app for this place was actually pretty fun."

I smile, remembering the way we curled up on the couch a couple weeks back, using his phone to pick colors for the walls we would never paint. Pretending for a night that this was a space we could keep.

When we get to the back door, I put a hand on his arm. There's music and voices coming from the other side. "Did you leave the TV on?"

The corner of his mouth turns up as he lets us in. "Nope."

The fumes hit me first, and then the shockingly

bright walls of a hall no longer marred by zebra-patterned paint and Old West runners. "Wha—?"

My feet won't move and a startled laugh slips past my lips. Because I don't understand what I'm seeing, can't wrap my head around the six guys from the team parked in Vaughn's living room.

My brother being one of them.

He's sprawled in the corner of the couch, Xbox controller in hand, shouting about how Julia never would have let some shot through. He looks like he's been there all day, and yet… I'm not getting a B&E-with-a-side-of-vandalism vibe off him.

"Greg," I choke out. "What are you doing here?"

He cuts a quick look my way and hands off the controller to Popov. "Hey, Nat. Yeah… so umm… We're hanging out, helping with some painting."

"*Painting?*"

He pushes his mouth around until it's finally muscled into something that looks like it's supposed to be a smile. "Because we're *friends*."

There is something so wrong with those words coming out of Greg's mouth. But then he's walking over to where we're standing to bust knuckles with Vaughn who asks if Julia made her flight okay.

I blink hard, wanting to be sure I'm actually seeing this. It's so civil. So surreal.

Greg shifts from foot to foot. "You guys want a beer?"

Quinn walks in from the kitchen with a few bottles

caught in his fingers and a streak of paint through his hair. "Step ahead of you. Hey, Natalie," he says, pulling me in for a one-armed hug.

I'm pretty sure my mouth is hanging open, but the guys are making easy conversation about the moves on the Xbox and what would have happened if Rux played that way during the last game. Greg laughs, and there's a crinkle at the corner of Vaughn's eyes. Eyes that keep cutting over to mine like he doesn't know exactly how I'm going to react.

Is this some kind of going-away gift? Like he wants to be good with the team that means so much to me before we leave for Oregon?

Vaughn takes me by the hand and leads me out to the patio. "Bet you never thought you'd see the day your brother and I made peace, huh?"

I give in to a quiet laugh and shake my head. "I guess if I'd known you planned to do it, I wouldn't have doubted." This is a man people should know better than to count out. "But why?"

"Because Greg is important to you. And what's important to you is important to me."

I reach up and stroke his cheek. "You don't know how much that means to me."

Vaughn's phone pings and he goes stiff. Pulling back, he holds up a finger. "One sec, baby."

He checks his phone with a grin as a chorus of distant pings and chirps starts up. What the heck?

"What's going on?" Only, I'm pretty sure I know. *Oregon.*

Whoops and congrats sound from the guys inside.

"Looks like my contract has been finalized."

The air whooshes from my lungs and drawing another breath seems beyond my ability. Because *this is it.* This is why he invited everyone over. So why would they be painting—?

"Hey, Allie." He's giving me his hushed voice, the one that carries twice the impact of his loudest bellow. Knuckle tucked beneath my chin, he tips my head so I meet his eyes. "You gonna congratulate me on my new contract with the Slayers?"

I nod, overwhelmed even though I knew this was coming. Even though I'm beyond proud of him. "Congra— Wait, *the Slayers?*"

The corner of his mouth hitches up and he tucks an arm around my back, pulling me in against the warm, solid planes of his chest. "Yeah, it took some convincing, but the Slayers have picked me up for another two seasons. I mean, a trade is possible. But I've made it clear I'm hoping to finish my career out here… in Chicago."

"B-but you hate Chicago. You hate playing with my brother," I add quietly, even though Greg's not close enough to hear… and he knows how Vaughn feels anyway.

"Chicago's grown on me. And your fu— your *brother* isn't so bad."

"Garcia?"

"I talked to him before everything went down. He was disappointed, but he got it. He's happy for me."

"Vaughn." I press my forehead into the center of his chest, dizzy and clinging to the one thing that matters. "How?"

Yes, he's a top scorer, but this is the guy who nearly got scratched from the lineup because of how poorly he fit in with the team. And now he's signed for two years? It doesn't make sense.

He chuckles into my hair, gathering me closer with those big strong arms. "Haven't you learned? If something's important to me… I'm *relentless*. And Allie, there's nothing more important to me than you."

I'm soaking his shirt with my tears but I swear I can feel him smiling above me.

"You didn't think I could do it, did you?"

I blink up at him. "Do what?"

"Prove that I could put you first."

I didn't. Not like this. I wouldn't have asked him to.

He sobers. "Hockey is a big part of my life. I've made sacrifices and paid dues and played like it was the only thing that mattered. But you've got to believe me when I tell you it's not."

"Vaughn, is this what you want?" I don't even know if it's possible to change it, but—

"Baby, never doubt it."

I nod, not sure I can speak.

"So what do you think? Want to keep this place?

The guys helped me out by painting it with the colors we picked, but only so you could see how you felt about it." He puts his hands on his hips, looking around like he didn't just turn his life upside down. *For me.* "I'm seeing some potential. But it's up to you."

And now I'm laughing, looking around through watery eyes… at our home. "I love it."

This time the smile that breaks past his scowl shatters it, leaving that broody demeanor in the dust. And his smile is beautiful. Overwhelming. And the predecessor to a kiss that steals my breath and turns my knees to jelly.

My arms lock around his neck and then he's pulling me against him so my toes leave the ground. He's kissing me like he'll never stop. And—

A throat clears behind us and we freeze, mouths fused, arms tight around each other. I crack an eye and find Rux standing where I'd expect my brother to be. His arms are crossed over his massive chest and there's a distinctive splotch of red across each cheek.

Oops.

"Yeah, so your brother just decided to take a quick jog around the block. He's uuh… totally happy for you." His eyes cut to Vaughn's and then back to mine. "If you're happy. But maybe try to keep it PG around him… you know, for a while."

Vaughn breaks from the kiss completely and threads his fingers through mine. "I can wait. Not like I'm going anywhere."

Rux's eyes flick down to our locked hands, his brows knit into an uneasy frown. "Yeah, I guess that'll be okay."

The poor guy isn't joking, but half the room starts laughing, me included. And when Greg shows up ten minutes later, I can see the struggle in his eyes before he mutters his congrats and pushes a stiff smile to his face.

Vaughn gives my hand a squeeze before letting it go. "I'm going to start the grill. O'Brian, want to give me a hand out here?"

"Yeah, man." Then to me, he asks, "Your friend George coming over?"

I don't have time to answer before Vaughn cuts in with a grumbled, "Jesus, Quinn, for the last time, she's not into you."

No. She's definitely not. And after what she told me, can't say I blame her.

Vaughn pulls me in, and the kiss he drops at my cheek has my heart doing flip-flops. It's tender and sweet. Easy. Like it's the most natural thing in the world. And I can't believe this is what my life looks like.

A hand settles on my shoulder, solid and warm. Greg. "This what you want, Goon?"

I can't help but smile at the decades-old nickname and the guy who wouldn't let me shake it. "Yeah, this is what I want."

"He still might get traded. You know how it works. The game always comes first."

"Not always." Not when it matters most. And that's

what I needed to know… what I never thought he or anyone would be able to convince me of.

"Yeah, guess not. I don't know a lot of guys who would take that kind of pay cut or go through the shit he did to make this work. He says he loves you." He's looking at me like I'm about to take the car out for my first solo spin. "And I can see you love him."

"I do," I say, smiling into my beer.

He nods. Arms stacking higher across his chest, eyes going hard as he juts his chin toward Vaughn. "You want a ring?"

That beer wasn't supposed to go into my lungs. After a few hacks, I gawk at my brother, but he's already laughing, backing away with his hands up. "Gotcha. I'll let you guys figure that out yourself."

…And we do.

Six months later in Vancouver, in the hotel that started it all. I wake up in the very same bed I snuck out of almost two years before. Vaughn is lying beside me, a gorgeous sparkling ring pinched between his fingers and that sexy smile on his always-a-little-rough face.

He opens his mouth, but I cut him off with my kiss, and when we come up for air, that ring is on my finger and I say the most wonderful word ever spoken.

"*Yes.*"

Thank you for reading DIRTY SECRET! Want a bit

more of Vaughn and Natalie? Keep reading for your
bonus epilogue and a sneak peek at Chapter one of
DIRTY HOOKUP

Vaughn

"ALLIE, we don't need to go," I offer, sitting up in bed to
watch as my fiancé of six months moves around our
room dressed in my T-shirt and a pair of panties. It'd be
sexy as hell if it weren't for the hand she's pressing to
her stomach. Sure, this wedding planning is important,
but I don't like that every time she has to sit down to
face it, she looks a little sick. "There's time."

She gives me a pitying smile and shakes her head.
"Not really. I know the big day isn't for another six

months, but since our invites outgrew the ballroom we booked, we've got to figure out where the heck we're going to have this thing. And Julia's leaving town again tomorrow. So this is our window."

"I get it." I just don't love it. And truth? The only reason I care about any of this wedding stuff at all is that Natalie cares about it. She wants it, therefore, I want it.

Bending my knees, I lean forward and wave her over with one hand. "Come back to bed for a minute."

She raises one pretty brow, and I huff out a laugh. "I'll be good. Promise."

Her lips curve into the smile that gets me every time, and she crawls into the space between my legs, tangling her fingers with mine. "I'm fine. I'm just a little anxious. But it's going to be worth it."

"Yeah, you excited?"

"I'm excited to finally be *your wife*."

My wife. Damn, I love the sound of that.

And maybe it's that low rumble coming from deep in my chest that gives it away, because Natalie's smile takes on some mischief and she bites her lip.

"I'll be *Mrs. Natalie Vassar*."

I gulp.

That's so hot. I can't fucking wait to have her wearing my last name.

But I said I'd be good, so, bad as I want to pull her onto my lap and make her say it again and again and again… I don't. Julia's helping us out in no small way with the planning and we shouldn't be late.

Natalie holds up our joined hands and wiggles the finger with my rock on it. "We'll have matching bands. Wide. Solid. *Platinum*. One look and everyone will know," She leans a little closer, peering up at me through the dark fringe of her lashes. "I'm *yours*."

Fuck me. I tried, but this girl knows exactly how to dirty talk me past restraint. In the next blink, I've got her flipped on her back, the weight of my body resting at the spread of her bare legs.

"I thought you were going to be good," she murmurs softly, fingers playing in my hair, the press of her heel at the back of my thigh telling me I'm exactly where she wants me to be.

"Oh, I'll be good." I brush my mouth against hers, teasing until she's breathless, arching beneath me, her lips parted in a plea I can't refuse. Fisting my hand in her hair, I give in to the crushing kiss I've been holding back.

She moans around the thrust of my tongue and slides her hand down to rub over my straining cock. And then the few clothes between us go and we're rolling around like it's the first fucking time we've been together in a year.

I can't get enough of her body, her quiet cries, and the look in her eyes when I push full length into her tight heat. *Nothing better*.

"So good," she pants, her hands skating over my

chest and shoulders. "Love this." Her eyes meet mine. "Love you."

I'm still not used to it. Every time she says those words, it's like a gift that takes my fucking breath away.

"Love you, baby. So much." I rock into the cradle of her hips, change the angle and watch as her lips part on a silent gasp and her knees slide higher up my ribs.

That's the spot.

I play there, working it with thrust after thrust. Taking her harder. Faster.

"Give it to me, Allie."

And then she's coming apart around me, crying out my name and dragging me along to release with her.

An hour later we're showered and changed and only ten minutes late getting over to her brother's place. That anxious look is back on her face and I'm half tempted to kiss it right off her in the elevator. Thing is, Baxter looks like he wants to lay me out every time I get within breathing distance of his sister as it is. So instead of making love to Natalie's mouth until she's half climbing me, I give her hand a squeeze and lean in to kiss the top of her head.

The elevator opens into the apartment half the team covets. It's a sweet place, huge, with a great view of the city. Only problem is the guy standing there to greet us.

Baxter gives me a tight smile—because we're friends now—and then pulls Natalie in for a warm hug. "Julia's turned the dining room into wedding central. You ready for this?"

For a second Natalie pales and a part of me wants to pull her aside and ask again if this is really what she wants. But then Julia steps out of the kitchen, phone at her ear.

"Send the contracts over and I'll look at them tomorrow. I'm off the rest of the day." She disconnects and rushes over for a couple quick hugs hello and then a kiss for her husband where she kind of melts into him.

When they come up for air, Baxter's got a kind of dopey look in his eyes that makes me dislike him a little less.

Julia takes a deep breath, rubbing her hands together. "Okay, guys, the clock's ticking. Let's do this thing."

Natalie

MY SISTER-IN-LAW IS INTENSE. I don't even know how long we've been at it, but Greg and Vaughn have been making phone calls and crossing off line items from the enormous white board all morning. They're neck and neck for who's accomplished more, and I'm a little worried about what's going to happen when one of them "wins."

Julia's sitting to my right, her ginormous binder

open between us and an array of brochures spread across the table.

"I love the Henley," she says, pointing to a picture of the rooftop rose garden. "But their ballroom isn't big enough for the reception and in the middle of winter…"

"Right," I agree, hit again by that same uneasy stomach from this morning.

She moves to the next hotel and then pauses. "Hey, you don't look so good."

Vaughn stops mid-call, turning to me. "Allie?"

I wave him off. "Hungry, I think. I probably should have had more than toast for breakfast."

He tells whoever's on the other end of the call he'll get back to them and hangs up. "Want me to pick up some grub—what sounds good?"

A minute ago, anything. But now? *Whoa.*

Greg ends his call. "You okay, Goon? Looking a little green around the gills."

I bite my lip, willing the lurch and roll in my belly away.

Pushing back from the table, I shake my head. "I'm just going to grab a glass of water. But order whatever you're up for."

Only when I stand the room starts going brown around the edges and the floor dips.

Vaughn's already moving, but it's too late. I'm going down.

NINETY MINUTES LATER, I'm still sour.

"I did *not* need the hospital," I grouse, but the two giants standing beside my bed with arms crossed aren't hearing it.

"Baby, you passed out," Vaughn says, eyes stricken as he looks me over.

Greg nods. "You don't even know what's wrong with you. And we're already here, so just sit tight and wait for the nice doctor to come and tell us what's wrong."

I look to Julia who's kicked back in the chair in the corner, hoping she'll see reason. "The only thing wrong with me is that I need a sandwich."

Sympathetic eyes meet mine. "I tried to stop them, but once they started fighting over who got to carry you to the car, there was no reasoning with them."

"I so did not need to be carried." Too bad my over-protective fiancé wasn't in a good place to listen.

Vaughn looks to Greg and for the first time, maybe ever, the two men I love most in the world don't look like they want to tear each other apart. "Maybe she oughta stay the night. Just to be safe."

"Overnight? It's two p.m.!" I squeak. I have no idea what happened in that dining room, but my money's on wedding stress and starvation. Though honestly, I've never been affected by stress like that before. But still.

Greg rolls his eyes. "Overnight is a good idea. We'll talk to the doctor about it."

Vaughn's shooting anxious looks my way and then reaching out to touch my leg, my hand, my hair like he thinks he's never going to be able to again. "Maybe I ought to get a nurse or someone for the house."

"Vaughn, *I'm fine*."

Julia starts to laugh. "I'm betting you are. But this is what you get for scaring the life out of all of us."

The door to our room opens and the doctor walks in. She's a tiny little thing who looks like she eats guys like Greg and Vaughn for breakfast. "That's it. Everybody out."

The guys start to argue, but Julia grabs Greg by the sleeve and pulls him out.

Vaughn's about to have a coronary and I'd rather he hear I'm fine from the doctor himself, so I ask if he can stay.

"Entirely up to you," she answers, setting a laptop on the small desk in the corner.

I start with the obvious. "I was just a little hungry and stressed out. Seriously, I know this is nothing."

She cocks her head. "Well, I wouldn't say *nothing*. When was your last period?"

I blink.

Vaughn blinks.

And then he coughs, takes a staggering step backward and drops, *grinning*, onto the bed beside me. "*Allie*."

But I'm shaking my head, looking from my fiancé to the doctor and back again.

"No," I say with a laugh that sounds a little like I might be choking. But she's got to understand. "We're *really* responsible about birth control."

"Natalie." He takes my hand.

"Okay, *mostly* really responsible. I mean, I stopped taking the pill so once we were married..." Except then I'm thinking about it more and just this morning, we didn't even stop to think about protection. "Vaughn?"

He's nodding, the smile on his face as wide as I've ever seen it. "Baby, let's give the doctor a minute before we get too excited."

My heart's racing and my belly feels like it's filled with butterflies. I look into the eyes of the man I love with everything I am and realize I'm already excited. "*Pregnant?*"

The doctor clears her throat. "That's what the lab results indicate. And ummm…"

But Vaughn's already pulling me into his lap, kissing my eyes, my cheeks, and my mouth. "A baby. *Our* baby."

This time the doctor laughs and lets out a sigh. "How about I give you two a minute and then we'll get a few tests run to see where we are in the timeline."

She lets herself out of the room and we're alone.

Smoothing the hair back from my face with a gentle touch, he searches my eyes. "Are you okay with this?"

"It's a surprise, yes. And a little sooner than we'd planned. But… *yes.*" I start to laugh and maybe cry a little too, but those tears are pure joy. And then we're kissing, holding each other and—

I break away, breathless. "Oh my God, Vaughn, do you know what this means?"

He glances back at the door. "Yeah, your brother is going to kill me for real."

I shake my head, my smile growing to cheek cramping proportions. "It means… we can *elope*!"

"Oh hell, *yes*." His smile matches mine and when he kisses me, it's filled with all the love and promises of our future. Eventually, he pulls back. His voice is low and gruff, filled with emotion. "*Tomorrow*. Let's elope tomorrow."

I nod. "I don't want to wait another day."

"Say it, baby."

This man. "*Mrs. Natalie. Vassar.*"

Available Now

One look and I know… this chick hates me.

265

I should walk away, find some puck bunny to gleefully sit on my lap and tell me what a big, hot, hockey stud I am--totally true, BTW. But there's just something about this feisty redhead I can't let go. She's got an edge to her that's sexy as hell and a smart mouth that's been tying me up since the night I met her.

She tells me to forget it, we're not happening. But this isn't the kind of woman a guy ever forgets. Especially when the air starts to sizzle and pop every time we get within ten feet of each other. She's in my head and under my skin, and all I can think about is the way she looked at me that one time. Like she already knew how it could be between us.

I'm not the kind of guy a girl like her takes home… But maybe I want to be.

One-Click **DIRTY HOOKUP** here!

DIRTY HOOKUP Chapter One Preview

Quinn
Last Season

That's it. No more bunnies.

One time I end up handcuffed to a bed with a missing key and, months later, I still haven't lived it down.

Trashing the latest gif—this one courtesy of the GM's wife—I glare at the hospital vending machine and the precariously balanced paper cup filled with coffee. This is gonna hurt.

Bending to retrieve the cup is bad enough but coming back up has me breaking out in a cold sweat. Everything aches. My knuckles are swollen and split. My shoulder feels like someone tried to yank my arm out of the socket. And my knees—damn, guys, sorry.

What a shit show.

We knew going in this game would be rough. Even without a team grudge like the one we were up against tonight with the Epics, hockey is a physical sport. You don't get on the ice without understanding there are risks inherent to the game. But Christ, it isn't Thunderdome.

Now we've got two of our best players in the hospital, and the fuck-face who started it from the other team getting stitched up across town. It's the kind of night that makes me envy the players who have someone to go home to. Someone real. Someone they trust to listen to how messed up things got.

Yeah, having a someone would be nice right about now.

But still… *no bunnies*.

I heave a breath and round the corner to the semiprivate waiting room where Greg Baxter, my team captain, texted that his little sister is currently freaking out. What he didn't mention is she's not alone.

Holy shit.

Coffee hot enough to melt the skin off my fingers sloshes over the rolled paper lip as I forget how to walk, every cell in my body tuning in to the redhead with a gentle hand on Nat's arm.

Her hair is this short spill of fiery waves around her face. And *that face*. I swear my heart just threw in an extra beat. My feet are moving double time. It's like I can't see the rest of her fast enough.

She's not as tall as Nat, but I'd bet my left nut she's an athlete. There's something about the stance, confident and alert. She's got a Foo Fighters T-shirt on that fits just right, and her cargo pants hint at strong legs and a phenomenal ass beneath.

Her arms and face are covered in pale freckles, and her lips are full and wide. I can't see her eyes yet, but with every step closer I know I'm about to. I want to. *I need to*.

Time fucking slows and I feel each heavy pump of my heart. A smile I can't quite explain starts pulling at my lips.

And then I have it—eye contact.

Those honey-browns meet mine, and something that feels a lot like recognition slams into me with the force of a two-hundred-pound defenseman. Only I've never seen this girl before. The way her eyes flare tells me that hinky sense of *something* isn't one-sided.

Her lips part, and I wait for the smile that answers my own.

This is the moment we'll tell our grandkids about. One look and I knew—

Whoa.

That's not a smile. In fact, that lush little playground has firmed into a flat line as unwelcoming as anything I've seen before. And those heart-and-soul eyes are suddenly hard as stone, narrowing fast.

Natalie notices me then and I nod, handing over the coffee as I get my shit together and try not to gawk at the girl whose pissy stare is practically daring me to engage.

Hospital, dipshit.

I'm here for Nat.

Only this girl is so intense, I can't be chill. I offer my hand. "Hi, I'm Quinn O'Brian. Don't think we've met before."

She doesn't take it, instead raising a brow as she asks, "Sure you'd remember if we had?" Her voice is husky and low, stroking softly against the back of my brain, like she's somehow managed to scratch at the fringe edge of some hard-to-reach itch. But then her words register, and I get it.

Shit. She already knows who I am. And not just the hockey stuff.

"Reputation's that bad, huh?" I ask, rubbing my neck with a sheepish grin.

I know it is. I've seen the posts. The polls. The bunnies running at the mouth about every Chicago Slayers player they've scored and the frequency with which my name comes up. It's never bothered me before.

Now?

I want to tell her whatever she's heard isn't true. That it's exaggerated… but I'd be lying. And before I can come up with a joke or even think to ask her name, she tells Nat she's got a call to make so her family doesn't worry.

She's *that* kind of girl.

It makes me smile because I like it, even if knowing she's that kind of girl means she's even further out of my league than she was ten seconds ago.

I watch her take off and then turn back to Natalie who's the reason I'm standing here. I won't ask her about her friend tonight. Hell, with the way that girl looked at me, all pissy indignation, I shouldn't ask about her at all.

But damn, I know I will.

***

George

Unfreakingbelievable.

Ducking around a corner, I press my back to the

wall and suck one shaky breath after another until the spots behind my eyes finally clear, along with any wayward thoughts about a third Slayers hockey player needing a bed in the ER.

I can't believe it. After all these years.

Quinn O'Brian.

Two feet in front of me. Giving me that same smile. The one that put my belly into free fall the first time I saw it. Left me breathless. And then less than a day later, left me humiliated. Devastated. Working up fantasies about the wrath I'd rain down on him if I ever saw him again.

So much for that badassery. My knees barely held me when I looked up to find those stupid sea-green eyes twinkling back at me like some Disney hero come to life.

Stupid eyes.

Stupid shoulders and muscles-everywhere body.

Stupid sandy blond hair standing up like some foolish girl had just had her hands in it for the last hour.

And that introduction.

Blowing out a breath, I shake my head.

He didn't even recognize me. Though why I ever thought he might is beyond me. Six years later and I'm still reading more into that night than there ever was...

One-Click DIRTY HOOKUP here!

———

Want to stay in the know about all my new releases?

Sign up for my **newsletter** and follow me on **BookBub**.

Also, you're invited to join the party! **Click here to get in on all the fun with my reader group, Mira Lyn Kelly's Book Bunnies**—we'd love to have you :-)

Also by Mira Lyn Kelly

SLAYERS HOCKEY

DIRTY SECRET (Vaughn & Natalie)

DIRTY HOOKUP (Quinn & George)

DIRTY REBOUND (Rux & Cammy)

DIRTY TALKER (Wade & Harlow)

DIRTY DEAL (Axel & Nora)

DIRTY CHRISTMAS (Noel & Misty)

DIRTY GROOM (Diesel & Stormy)

DIRTY D-MAN (Bowie & Piper)

DIRTY DARE (Gulls & Cam)

DIRTY FLIRT (Boomer & Lara)

DIRTY FIGHTER (Static's Story)

BACK TO YOU

HARD CRUSH (Hank & Abby)

DIRTY PLAYER (Greg & Julia)

DIRTY BAD BOY (Jack & Laurel)

THE DARE TO LOVE NOVELS

TRUTH OR DARE (Tyler & Maggie)

TOUCH & GO (Sam & Ava)

Acknowledgments

Writing is a team sport. I couldn't do it alone. I wouldn't want to. And I am beyond grateful, every single day, for the girls who make sure I never feel like I am.

So THANK YOU...

First, to Lexi Ryan, for being my sounding board, willing ear, voice of reason, chatty break buddy, closest confidant, plot whisperer and a million other things. But mostly for *being there*. Thank you for being my bestie and being who you are. I love you!

To Lori Rattay, who seriously saved my butt this year, chats books and ideas with me, and is one of the sweetest girls I know! To Lisa Kuhne who knows everything, never judges my need to spoil my dogs, and makes me snort laugh on the regular. To Jessica Alcazar for putting up with my crazy despite my refusal to do this ONE THING she wants lol. To Annika Martin for the lunch dates and glitter mishaps and always being the amazing person she is! To Holly Mortimer (@thesocialvert) for always answering my frantic calls and being so generous with her limitless know-how. And to

Jennifer Haymore who has been along for this ride from the very first days.

To Zoe York, Elle Rush, Adriana Anders, Brighton Walsh, Kait Nolan and all my friends over in Slack who make sprinting to the finish fun. To Molly O'Keefe, R.L. Kenderson, Jane Ashley Converse, K.C. Enders, Jennifer Ann, Helene Cuji, and Crystal Perkins for all the laughs, cheers and book talk. To all the girls from the PJ Party, my awesome eagle eye readers, and the bloggers and reviewers who help spread the word about my books.

To the girls over at Give Me Books Promotions and Najla Qamber Designs and my agent Nicole Resciniti.

To my family who puts up with my crazy hours and pig pen office.

And especially to you! Thank you for reading.

((HUGS)) Mira

About the Author

Hard core romantic, stress baker, and housekeeper non-extraordinaire, Mira Lyn Kelly is the USA TODAY bestselling author of more than a dozen sizzly love stories with over a million readers worldwide. Growing up in the Chicago area, she earned her degree in Fine Arts from Loyola University and met the love of her life while studying abroad in Rome, Italy… only to discover he'd been living right around the corner from her back home. Having spent her twenties working and playing in the Windy City, she's now settled with her husband in rural Minnesota, where their four amazing children and two ridiculous dogs provide an excess of action and entertainment. www.miralynkelly.com

Looking to stay in touch and keep up with my new releases, sales and giveaways?? Join my newsletter and Facebook reader group at MiraLynKellyPJParty. We'd love to have you!!

Printed in Great Britain
by Amazon